GREGORY EL HARVEY

THE PATTERN OF A SNOWFLAKE

A NOVEL

Books by Gregory El Harvey

JACKSONVILLE

Autobiographical
FACES IN THE SHADOWS

Serial
THE PATTERN OF A SNOWFLAKE
DRAGONS MORE DECENT THAN MEN
DRAGONS IN LOVE
TO DIE IN THE COLDEST WINTER
THE AUTONOMOUS ASSASSINS

Cover painting: *Seven Moons Over the Hill*
by Gregory El Harvey
(www.gregharveygallery.com)

To those who fall in love.

ACKNOWLEDGMENTS

I am grateful to Myanna Harvey for reading the manuscript, to Cassia Harvey for helping with the publication process, and to my best friend Tai Ping for often sitting with me throughout the night.

CHAPTER 1

Philadelphia, December 2007

Stanley Osipov pulled his wire-rims down and looked above them to read a grievously small DVD title. He had tried bifocals some years earlier, but finding them more annoying than helpful, had resolved simply to move things out of the way.

"They're mixed up, aren't they?" came a woman's voice from the next aisle.

Pushing the glasses up, he peered inquisitively over the top shelf. "I am sorry?"

"I said they're jumbled, the titles."

He could not but look at the blond hair. Then he replied, "Yes, they are, yes, mixed."

She smiled at his Russian accent. "Christmas shoppers, I think. Everything in the store is mixed up. I can't seem to find anything. And there's not a lot left to choose from."

He did not want to stare, but found himself doing so. The hair was a radiant platinum and the eyes a piercing gray. The face overall was remarkably attractive. No, he did not want to stare, but he had never been very good at turning away from beauty. His gaze alternating between her hair and her eyes, he finally said, "I have noticed that, yes."

"Noticed what?"

He hesitated. "Well, . . . what you said."

"That there wasn't much to choose from, or that I couldn't find what I was looking for?"

"Uh, no, the first one, that there is not much to pick from."

"Ah, otherwise, you might have been watching me, right?"

"Yes, I suppose that is correct," he replied cautiously, looking at her hair again. He had not realized until then that it was shoulder length. He thought she might be Swedish or even German. She seemed quite mature, perhaps in her late forties or early fifties.

With a faint smile she asked, "What are you looking for?"

He hesitated. "What?"

"Movies. What movie are you looking for? Maybe it's on this side, Comedies and Romance."

"Well, this is Documentaries. But actually, *The Guns Of August.*"

"Oh, Fritz Weaver. No, I don't think I've seen it over here. I'll come around."

As she turned the corner, entered his aisle, and walked toward him he took in her full form and the way she walked. He saw instantly the natural symmetry but also refinement to her form that even the long wool coat could not neutralize. She was tall and thin and had an aura, a pathos, that made

2

him think of the women of Warsaw and Berlin. He could not have given an accurate count of the women he had photographed in his career, but there had always been something different about each of them. Each of them had some mystique, some way of displaying to the universe the Divine fingerprints. He had never comprehended the claim of some photographers that all women were the same through a lens. They never seemed the same to him. And if he came to know them, they never seemed to be the same in spirit either. It was as if nature demanded a different category for every woman he had ever known. And this woman too, this tall, mature woman, with her elegant walk, platinum hair, confident eyes, seemed unique. Turning fully to face her as she approached, he looked straight into the cool, gray eyes.

"Thanks for coming around," he said. He wanted to say more, but left it at that.

"That's quite all right," she replied unemotionally. "I don't mind."

"Most people would not have heard of the movie," he said, "but you even knew the narrator? How should that work?"

"I believe the idiom is 'how *does* that work'."

"Yes," he replied quickly, recoiling. "Sorry."

Thinking for a moment that her correction had been unwise, she said nonchalantly, "Sure. I'm not really into war, but that was a good movie. You've seen it, right?" She wondered whether, after all, he did look to be in his late fifties, for she had thought that he would look younger. She could see that he was lean, though, perhaps too lean, and had been handsome in his youth.

"Oh, yes, I have seen it, yes. I got it from the library. But I thought I might get the inexpensive copy to own, you know."

He could see now that she was at least in her fifties, extremely well preserved. He sensed a frailty in her that somehow reminded him of Europe; not just of the women he had known there—yes, certainly of them—but of Europe itself, or herself, the continent that had both waged and suffered war, it seemed, for all of time. And so he sensed a strength too, a strength that, like that of Europe, might survive the erosive effects of time. And he saw in the gray eyes remarkable depth and intelligence, a nobility, again, like that of a Europe that might rule the world.

"Well, we can look," she said.

Reading this as more intentional than charitable, he hesitated, but then said, "This is fine, but I don't want to cause you any troubles." Not from nervousness but simply from habit he put both hands half way into the pockets of his jeans and with his elbows momentarily pressed the sides of his leather coat against his ribs. Of course, this made his shoulders rise in an apparent shrug, when he hadn't meant to shrug at all.

"Be hopeful," she continued, ignoring his protest, "and maybe we can find it. I doubt they'd have it in the back, since they're closing out."

"No, I think you are correct," he agreed. And then, shifting his weight to the other foot, another habit, acquired from considering posed subjects at length, he tried again. "But I don't want to bother you with it. It is okay. I will look for a little while more and then just give it up. I didn't mean to take you away from your own shopping. I am sorry."

She noted his sincerity. "It's all right, don't worry. I've got some time, I'm not in a hurry." And immediately she began to look through the titles on the shelf, moving the cases with her fingers. "So, you like war movies or just documentaries?"

He was fascinated by the combination of maturity and youth in her. There was something convincing, seductive in the combination, which worked, he thought, like a good photograph worked. The artificial didn't matter, and you looked past it, but if you took it away altogether, the magic was lost. He could hear and see that she was not a smoker. He guessed she might even be into herbs and nature, yet she carried herself in a distinctly metropolitan manner. At length he answered, "Actually, both are good. I like documentaries, I am a documentary fan, but I like animals and nature too."

She gave him a glance, noting his simple demeanor, that he had said it as a child would say it. She had learned to dismiss such disarming characteristics, so she said quickly, "Nature and war are not the best of bedfellows."

"You are correct, I admit it. They do not go together, and war is very bad."

"What nature things do you like?"

"I have watched the English things, it was a series. I actually do not remember. It was from the library."

"You must spend a lot of time there."

He grinned. "No, I watched them at home."

5

She shot him a look for the levity. "Cute, very cute."

"One of the episodes was about the melting ice of the Antarctic. A polar bear was swimming out to find food, I remember, and it was very tragic and sad."

He did not help in the search, but watched her as she continued looking through the titles. He noted that she wore no ring. But of course, that might mean any number of things. He was beginning to enjoy himself. It seemed entirely appropriate for her to take over the project, and he contented himself with simply backing out of her way.

Suddenly she stopped, straightened herself, and pronounced that the film was not there, not on that shelf anyway. She turned to look at him squarely and saw that the stubble on his face was quite attractive. The closely cropped gray hair, which was almost gone on the top, seemed in perfect balance with his head. Yes, he had been handsome in his youth, but probably he had charmed no one, for clearly he did not have the bearing of a charmer. He was pathetic, she decided, and pathetic people, she knew, never intentionally charmed anyone. Father had been like that. He had been good and true, and perhaps a little too candid when he spoke, so that Mother, fearing he might say too much, would sometimes suggest he might keep his mouth shut. Yes, Father had been naive, pathetic, and could never have charmed anyone.

Her hair seemed to be picking up every ray of light in the store. Transfixed, he said, "Maybe someone moved it."

With a little smile, she returned, "I did say that to begin with, didn't I? That's what *mixed up* means." And when he just looked sheepish at this, she added, "Maybe, we should go back to Comedies and Romance and give it a good look there."

"Why would it be there?"

She shrugged. "Could be, someone picked it up here and when they got to the good movies dumped it."

"Like in Comedies and Romance?"

She smiled again. "Well, sex is always better than war, don't you think?"

"But you said you thought it was a good movie."

"Oh, it was. I enjoyed its quality and philosophy. I wouldn't want to see it repeatedly, but then, that war was kind of like that."

"Like what?"

Impatiently she returned, "Well, somewhat lacking in comedy and romance, wouldn't you say?"

When she added a pretty smile, as if half to poke fun and half to make peace, he saw that her teeth, clean but unwhitened, corroborated his last surmise of her age, so he ventured a more specific guess of sixty-two. He answered amicably, "Yes, you are correct again. It was definitely not a funny or sexy war."

"Yeah, a bad one," she whispered playfully.

"Attrition."

"Like this conversation."

He enjoyed spontaneous humor, but had not engaged in it for a long time. He found her speech delicious and wanted to hear her say something else. When she did not he offered clumsily, "The film has great footage though, some very beautiful shots. I love black and white. Do you like black and white, or just color?"

"You're a photographer?" she asked abruptly, but then thought she had asked too soon. When he nodded, she said quickly, "Just a guess."

"That was a good guess, a very good guess."

Continuing her caprice, she asked, "So, are you freelance?"

"Yes."

"Are you a bit of a rogue, or have I watched too many movies?"

"I think, too many movies. Most photographers are really just in love with cameras—cameras and lenses and tripods, and of course, images." Then, with a nod toward the movies in her hand, he queried, "What movies did you get?"

"From the good section?" she teased, but then held up before him the two cases, one in each hand. Looking askance at him, she asked, "Do you approve?"

He leaned closer. "*Tom Jones*. Yes, I do approve," he said. "That was very good, I saw it. And *The Goodbye Girl*. I did not see this one, but I am sure you watch nice stuff." Having concentrated on improving his vernacular English of late, he felt proud of his use of this last word. "I have seen *Tom Jones* two times, and you have seen my movie, so I am lucky, yes? Maybe I should try to guess your profession."

"You might try."

"And if I succeed?"

"I am an English teacher, thank you." Placing the films together again, she extended her right hand. "I'm Martina," she said amiably with an overly flat American accent, and then with a heavy German accent and with raised eyebrows, "Martina Jung."

He gave a short, polite bow and shook her hand briefly. "Stanley Osipov. It is very nice to meet you."

"Oh, you can do better than that," she said brightly.

Thoroughly charmed now, he responded in his purest Russian, "Stanislav Osipov."

"Oh God, I love the Russians."

"And I, the Germans. We are both lying, right?"

They laughed at this, for they knew, as everyone does, that lies when they are understood and accepted can be like the truth and can lead to camaraderie and its joys. And so, they met and lied and laughed and after making her purchase left the store together and stood in the winter sunshine and could not find an easy way to part. When she grew chilled and suggested they go for coffee he was relieved, producing a stocking cap and pulling it on to ride just above his brow. She had left her car at home and walked, she said, for she lived in Lawncrest. He was delighted at this and walked her to his car, where he removed boxes from the passenger seat and brushed it off awkwardly. She could only say that it looked like a photographer's car and that it would be good just to get in and out of the cold. Once on Rising Sun Avenue, they drove toward the Adams intersection.

"Cold?" he asked, adjusting an air vent.

"Not really," she answered cautiously, but then, "Well, maybe a little, yes."

"I am sorry," he laughed, holding his hand to the vent. "It is on the highest level now, and this is all the work it is capable of. It is not doing very much work, is it?"

She shook her head.

"I had the heater repaired at a local garage, and the mechanic installed the incorrect heater core. It is for truck, not minivan. He said it was cheaper and did not think I would mind."

"Why don't you take it back?"

He shrugged. "It is life, I think."

Pulling her collar a little more snug, she asked if he repaired cars.

"I have done it, but many years ago, in Russia."

She glanced at his fingernails. It was her tendency to persist in confirming a description she had been given, regardless of how accurate it appeared to be. "So, you know about cars?"

"A little."

"Is this a good car?"

He chuckled. "I bought it used, but it is notorious for having transmission problems. I have had nothing but problems with it. I have put two rebuilt transmissions in it—$2,000 each. But it is wonderful to drive. I got it mostly for my equipment."

"Tripods?"

"Yes, tripods," he laughed. "I do not actually use a lot of tripods, but yes. There is a coffee shop in Jenkintown, where I stop sometimes. Would that be okay?"

"Of course. That would be lovely."

Then he said, "I heard on the news that the chairman of House Intelligence Committee said that he is going to ignore the request from Bush to stop investigating why CIA tapes were destroyed. Did you hear that?"

She moistened her lips. "No, I didn't hear that."

"But you have heard about it, right? It is on the news."

She cleared her throat. "Well, yes, a little."

"And what," he asked cheerily, "do you think about it?"

"I suppose I am noncommittal."

"Really?"

"Yes, really. What do you think about it?"

"I do not know. It is good, I think, to have some kind of peaceful—you know, I mean, legal—check for the way governments do things. If revolution is the only check, well, that seems ridiculous."

"I think I can agree with that," she returned, looking at his hands as he drove.

As this response seemed to be acceptable to him, she wondered whether it wouldn't be better just to draw him out right there, get him to talk while he was in the mood. She had always been good at timing, but then, one could always make a mistake. People were too complex, and the development of a relationship might be spoiled because of bad timing or even a misplaced word. She had played it fairly safe so far.

She had noticed him glancing at her legs, as if to discern their shape through her coat. Perhaps he was interested. He had seemed to like the way she looked. But then, looks were so important to a photographer, as if the image was pretty much all there was to reality. Her instinct told her he had found her to be attractive. She would know for certain in short order, but for now, yes, she was fairly sure about it. Usually she knew at the beginning, from the first moment of meeting, but sometimes not until things had progressed. If she doubted herself, she righted herself. But in the end, she knew, and after all, she had never been wrong. If the subject was attracted to her, she knew in what way, and if he wasn't, she knew exactly why. This one, this Mr. Osipov, had looked at her in a way that was definitely not asexual. But she must be discerning, for photographers often stared in that different way, which was not asexual, but where sensuality was so blended with a pure sense of beauty that the two interests were indistinguishable. Yes, he had looked at her, and she felt fairly certain that both interests were there.

And so it was not unnatural that their going for coffee lasted until mid-afternoon, or that he then asked her to an early dinner, or that at the restaurant they talked until it was so late that he had to apologize to the waiter for monopolizing the table. Yes, all was as it should have been in the meeting of Martina Jung and Stanley Osipov on that sunny Saturday in the middle of December.

"Thank you, Stanley," she said to him at her door after he had driven her home. "I took you for coffee and you took me to dinner. That was very nice. I had a good time, and I enjoyed the conversation. You're a man of many interests. It was lovely."

When she extended her gloved hand he shook it gently with his bare hand and said that he too had enjoyed himself and that he hoped to see her again.

"I'd like that," she said. After turning the key in the lock, she said simply, "Call me."

As he drove away he slowed to look at her front window, although he knew that such a woman would never be peeking after him. At least twice during the short drive to Olney he lowered his window for fresh air, as if to feed cold oxygen to the flames of his exhilaration.

When she had hung her coat in the closet, she stood for a moment in the solitude of the darkened room. The kitchen's faint light threw a golden haze into the room and shafts across the carpet, animating some of the tiny pagodas and the surrounding flowers and birds in the pattern. But false light often made inanimate objects seem organic. Then she flipped off the kitchen light and walked to the stairs. At the top Maggie opened her door and stood to look at her.

As if to a stranger, Martina said, "Yes?"

Maggie adjusted the pink towel that swathed her wet hair. "Everything all right, dear?"

"Yes, of course," she answered, collecting her thoughts. "It went well. Yes, everything's fine."

Pressinh the towel to her head, "I was just hoping for a few details."

"I'm a little tired."

"You look it, dear. But what do you think, is it a yes?"

"It is," she replied. "Are you finished in the bathroom?"

"Sure, sure, I'm done."

In half an hour, her teeth brushed, her face bathed, Martina slipped into a silver silk nightgown, pulled the covers back, and sat on the bed to check the setting on the alarm clock. Connecting the charging wire, she put her phone in its usual place, where she might reach it in the night. As she snuggled into the pillow she thought of him as she had first seen him in the next aisle that morning, then as she had watched him through the storm door that night. Yes, he had been handsome in his youth. She thought of his eyes behind the glasses as he had looked at her, at her hair, her legs. She thought of his voice, his candor, his sincerity. She thought of his intelligence—they had certainly been right about that.

CHAPTER 2

Early the next morning he arose quickly. Not bothering to reach for the thick, dirty robe he loved to wear on cold mornings, he went downstairs in underwear and bare feet, moved the thermostat up to sixty-four, and after hearing the heater's response from the basement, ran back up to the bathroom to wash.

The milk for the oatmeal was extra cold, and the coffee, its grounds still in the cup, was extra strong. It all reminded him of how he had eaten breakfast in Russia, except of course when he was at home. Then his mother Aglaya, like every good Russian mother, would try to turn him into a glutton. But he had resisted the endless loaves of bread and bowls of potatoes, for he did not want to become another slob Russian or imitate the big fat slob Americans he had seen. But he had learned from his father Alexsey the Terrible, as he was called in the family, that soldiers sometimes preferred to leave the grounds in the cup to make the coffee stronger. He had watched transfixed as Alexsey prepared cups and coffee and brought water to a rolling boil, and he had needed little else than the simple reference to the soldiers to paint the scene into his mind and color it into something exotically attractive. The coffee, however, as he often remembered first experiencing it, had not tasted exotic, but just plain good. Aglaya, who prided herself in being refined, had frowned at his lighted eyes and warned him that coffee prepared in such a way would kill him as quickly as vodka, and worse, dry his skin and make him *look* like a soldier. Alexsey had laughed, and he had laughed with him. He thought of them both now as he finished the oatmeal and sipped the gritty coffee. But he gave up the pleasant image when his cell rang and he saw Martina's name on its screen.

"Well, hi," he said simply.

"Stanley? Good morning."

"Good morning to you. Nice to hear your voice."

"Thank you. Listen, I don't know if you're busy today, but I was wondering if you would like to stop by at a party I'm giving for the holidays. There'll just be a few people I work with and a few friends and neighbors."

"Yes, I would love to come," he replied. "That would be very great, yes."

"It's casual, you can come as you are."

"What if I am less than casual?" he teased.

"Well, then, dress up." And when he laughed she added, "Just don't come naked."

"It will be very good, thank you. What time do you want me to come?"

"Oh, about twelve-thirty, why don't you?"

"I will get out of church about at that time, so is later okay?"

"Church," she repeated. Then after a moment she said, "Yes, certainly, that would be fine. Why don't you come as soon as you can, then."

When he had closed the phone he clasped it in his hand as a precious thing. In his youth in Russia he had clung to his empty tea mug not only for warmth, but also out of sentiment, because his mother had prepared the tea. Always he found himself clinging to the warm and the beautiful. Opening his fingers, he looked at the instrument and thought of Martina's voice, her lips, her warmth.

During the service at church he could not keep his gaze from a woman in the opposite balcony. Her shoulder-length platinum hair seemed very like Martina's. When the woman became aware of his attention and returned his gaze he looked away and tried to focus his mind upon the sermon.

Following the service he took his usual route west along the Schuylkill, exiting for U.S. 1. But instead of getting off at Broad, he took the Adams Avenue exit from the boulevard and eventually made a right onto Rising Sun. As he drove through Martina's neighborhood he tried to shake the idea that he was committing an error in not bringing a gift. After another block he parallel parked and walked the last quarter block to the house. He climbed the concrete steps, rang the doorbell, and took a step backward to look at the front of the house. The old granite façade was in good shape, and the window trim had been recently painted.

Although the house rested prominently at the end of a block and was somewhat wider than the other rows, it seemed to exhibit distinction without ostentation. In fact, without exception the other row houses on both sides of the street seemed well maintained and either bore a few simple holiday decorations or none at all. From his vantage point at the top of the steps the neighborhood seemed charming, even beautiful, in its cleanliness and smartness, and he breathed its winter air with a sense of security and peace.

When the inside door was opened the face of a woman with short, almost mannish brown hair appeared behind the glass of the storm door. Then the storm door was pushed open and he stepped inside. Her hair had been lightly oiled and combed back on both sides, giving her a distinctly aristocratic appearance, and he felt he might have seen her at any number of parties he had photographed along the French Riviera.

"Hello, Stanley?" she inquired cordially, closing the door and turning to him.

"Yes, hi," he replied.

She extended her hand. "I'm Margaret Swift-Jones. I live here with Martina."

Shaking the hand and looking into the green eyes, he said, "Yes. It's very nice to meet you. You teach with Martina, history, yes?"

"Exactly. And you are a photographer."

"Yes."

"Well, I'll take your coat. And just call me Maggie. My students call me Ms. Jones. If I do *Swift-Jones*, I get jokes, don't ask me why."

Stuffing his gloves into the pockets, he handed her the jacket and then stood watching as she went to hang it up. She had a beautiful, sensuous walk, crossing the oriental rug as much like something out of a jungle as a classroom. Clearly she had the body of an athlete, but the way she carried herself in the black half-heels, tight black pants and red-striped white shirt left little doubt of her sophistication. She seemed perfectly to combine the country club with the art studio. As she approached her emerald eyes alive with a fairy-tale light not unlike that of a crystal ball.

"Well," she offered, as if greeting him for the first time, "it's so nice you could come. And isn't it awful out? I hate the winter so much."

He wanted to hate it, too, after hearing her say it, but he said, "You are not a winter person, yes?"

"Good Lord, no. I was not exaggerating, believe me, I loathe the cold. It is an enemy." She threw her hands apart, as if to dismiss the whole business. "When everybody else is cheery over new fall fashions coming out, I'm still looking at swimsuits and dreaming of Bermuda."

His eyes following the Presley-cut hair, the luminous skin, he easily imagined her in a swimsuit, although not stretched out under a burning sun. Feebly he offered, "You are too white to be a serious sun worshipper, I think."

"Correct. I don't worship the sun, just its heat. The sun is very damaging, I know. And I don't hate the snow, only the cold, the wretched cold."

Mesmerized, he could only stare at her. She had an aloof, almost aristocratic charm about her that he was finding difficult to resist. Her nose was straight as a pencil and her teeth were pleasant and bright. It was a face, he thought, that begged to be photographed *ad infinitum,* not for money but for art. And there was a color in the skin that he could not define, a warm, seductive whiteness like that of a very expensive car. And no makeup—at least, that he could discern. He thought she might be in her late fifties.

"Yes," she continued, "but then, you're from Russia, I understand. The winter probably doesn't bother you at all." She shook her head and brought her hands together for emphasis.

His eyes left her to watch Martina coming down the stairs.

"Hi, Stanley," she said, offering her hand.

"Martina," he replied simply.

"Is Maggie showing you around?"

"I just got here. You have a beautiful house."

"Thank you," she said, patting him on the shoulder. "I like your sweater, very nice."

"Thank you. You look very nice, too. You both do." For just a moment he dropped his gaze, but then he looked up at her and let his eyes move over her face, her hair, her sweater. It seemed that her beauty was as real as it had been the previous day. He wondered whether the sorcery was still there, but he saw in her eyes and in her smile that it was.

"Thank you," she said again.

Maggie pressed her hands together again and offered a little melodramatically, "Oh, Martina, you've brought us a polite man."

They laughed, and he protested, "Now, now, have pity on a poor immigrant."

Hugging herself for warmth, Maggie queried, "What kind of camera does a polite photographer use?"

Martina touched his shoulder again. "Oh, yes, Maggie loves photography. You two will have to talk about lenses and things."

"You asked what kind of camera?" he repeated, confused by the query.

The green eyes shone mischievously. "Yes, it was a riddle. *What kind of camera does a polite photographer use?*"

Uncertain how to answer, he pushed his hands into his pockets. "I suppose," he ventured, "one with a powerful lens, so people will not know they are being photographed and so will not be offended."

The green eyes flashed with satisfaction. "Very good."

"Maggie's a capricious tease, I'm afraid," Martina chuckled. "She will drive you nuts. Maggie, stop playing with my friend." And taking his arm in hers, she said, "Everyone's in the kitchen and there's lots of food. Have you had lunch?" When he shook his head, she pitied him, wondering if tragedy in his life had hurt him. But she checked herself, gave the arm a squeeze, and started them toward the kitchen. "You have to eat, I insist. Come on, I'll introduce you."

He could feel the warmth from her body as they walked, and when they reached the kitchen he was glad she continued to hold him.

"Everyone," she announced from the doorway, "this is Stanley, a friend of mine."

As if practiced, the group paused their conversations and turned in greeting, bottles and cups cheerily aloft, and a mustached man, stepping forward with his hand out, said robustly, "Happy times, Stanley, I'm George, nice to meet you."

He shook the hand and nodded a smile to the others, then followed Martina to a table loaded with party food. As she prepared a sandwich for him he watched her hands.

"I hope you're hungry, Mr. Osipov."

He replied that of course he was, that the Russians were always hungry, but then felt sheepish that he had said something so stupid. She informed him as she made his sandwich that the meat was called Russian black bear ham and that she expected him to enjoy it. Nodding obediently, he took the loaded paper plate, but then felt very much alone when she walked away and left him. Then she returned and began talking to him.

"Everyone likes a kitchen," she said, clearly making conversation. "We had it expanded, and now it's about as large as the dining room." When he made no response, but stood simply, like a child, eating his sandwich, she leaned close and said to him softly, "I'm glad you came, I like having you here."

Then she left him again, but as she walked away she felt his eyes upon her body and in the doorway turned briefly and met his eyes with hers. Somehow she felt he knew she was going to the bathroom. When she returned to the kitchen she found that he had not moved.

"I'm sorry," she said. "Everything okay?"

He finished chewing, then answered, "Sure. I am glad to have you back. The sandwich is very good, yes."

"There's a lot of food here, so please help yourself."

"I will."

"Don't listen to her," came a very feminine voice beside him. "She'll make you fat. She's a nurturer, a German nurturer, do you believe it?"

"Oh, yes," Martina said, reaching to touch the woman's arm. "Gretchin Wheeler, Stanley Osipov. Gretchin, take care of him, will you? I need to get more cheese from the basement. See you in a minute, Stanley."

"So, you're a photographer, Martina says." She squinted at him suspiciously and posed yourself, waiting for his response.

"Yes, I am," he replied, uncertain whether he was expected to say more.

Beneath each of her sparkling aqua eyes was a prominent dot of blue-green body paint. Her smile, broad but not quite a grin, showed artificially whitened teeth. Long, red hair, in ringlets, surrounded her sensuous face, offering it like a plate of fruit. The fruit, however, was guarded by a slinking green dragon tattooed across the left side of her neck.

"And," she continued, "you are from Russia."

He nodded. "You are a teacher?"

She replied with a sensuous *uh-huh* and took a swig from her bottle of beer wrapped in a paper napkin.

Patiently he watched the bottle go up and come down. He thought she might be in her late forties.

After she had swallowed, he asked, "What do you teach?"

"Art. I teach art, traditional and modern. Drawing, painting, sculpture. Sculpture's a little heavy for public school, but I get it in. Soapstone's good, kids like cutting soapstone. Dust gets all over, though—it's horrible—kids track it over the whole school. But yeah, I teach general art. Sometimes I fill in for the music teacher. I like classical music, so I push it. The kids don't like it, though. Yeah, classical when I can get away with it, pop when I can't, you know." Then, as if she had just finished presenting a rehearsed speech, she closed her lips to form a pretty pout.

Wondering why she would do this with lipstick that was nearly black, he said, "Classical? I would have guessed *jazz*."

This seemed to give her a charge, and she became especially animated, saying things like oh hell, yeah, she loved jazz and Dave Brubeck and all of it, but always found herself coming back to classical music. She sort of swaggered in her talk, and he wondered why she made no attempt to seem more real. She said she was fairly versatile and could teach anything in the visual arts or in music.

Before taking another bite of the sandwich, he queried, "You teach at Martina's school?"

"Uh-huh," she breathed sensuously, delicately scratching just above her top button, watching his eyes. "Go on," she urged, "eat your sandwich, Stanley. There's a ton of food, and somebody has to eat it. I like to watch men eat, so I'll watch you. I'm not making you nervous, am I?"

He took a small bite of the sandwich, then asked, "Have you known her long?"

"About five years. She's kind of retired, but still teaches. Teaching's like that. Once you have tenure, and especially after you've been around awhile, nobody forces you out. You might have to teach something you don't like, but you can stay in the system for as long as you want. And she's pretty young at heart, so she'll be around for a few years. She's cool, and she gets a lot of respect too."

He wished he had been given a smaller sandwich. He did not mind eating *with* people, but he loathed eating for their entertainment. Accordingly he began to take smaller bites from the sandwich, until he eventually just dropped its remnants onto the plate and set everything on the counter beside him. For a moment they were silent, and he was relieved when Martina announced to everyone that there was more sliced cheese and the television was on, if anyone was interested. But when she did not come over to them he knew he must continue with the conversation.

"It is a good party, yes?" he offered.

Working her lips together for a moment, then moistening them with her tongue, tasting the lipstick, Gretchin merely cooed, "Oh yeah."

Annoyed with this display, he asked, "Do you want to watch the television?"

"But I like photography," she returned. "What do you photograph?"

He sighed to himself. "I usually work as an independent, for the major newspapers, yes."

"The big guys, that's interesting. But you're not in the system, that's great."

"They will call me to fill in for a staff photographer who is sick or drunk or something."

"But wouldn't you like to get on staff? Then you could get drunk and someone could fill in for you."

He shrugged. "I like working on my own, yes. Sometimes, if I get an interesting picture and they do not want it around here, I send it up to New York. I am not rich, but I like my work."

She followed his lips as he spoke, then asked, "But you do your own stuff, right? I mean, just for yourself?"

He nodded, uncomfortable under her salacious eyes.

"Do you ever," she continued, "do artsy stuff? You know, like, figures, nudes or anything?"

Slowly he shook his head. "Not really, I think."

"No boudoir stuff, huh?"

He looked at her face, the dark lips, the whitened teeth, then said, "Well, I did take some nudes about one month ago, on an assignment in the city."

"Yeah?"

"A woman, in her boudoir, as a matter of fact, had been shotgunned. No nose, no face, just meat and a lot of blood."

"Jesus."

"Actually," he returned, "she was beyond religious help."

She blinked. "I imagine."

Hoping he had shut her up, he looked toward the doorway. The eyes he wished to look into were not salacious.

Then she said, "I'd like to see your work sometime. Do you ever show?"

"Exhibit? No, not really. I mean, I have shown my photographs in exhibits, but not here. In Europe."

"How long have you been here?"

"For about five years."

"But your accent is quite American. I do pick up something though. But that's amazing. You must have a good grasp of language."

Shrinking before her pretentiousness, he replied simply, "I have worked on it. I did speak a little English before that."

"But your idiom is good. And do you speak any other languages?"

He shrugged. "Maybe a little German and French, maybe some Czech. But you are Swedish, yes?"

Silent for a long moment, she finally answered, "Well, I *was*." When he smiled she asked, "But how did you know that?"

"I was only asking it," he replied, noting that the sparkle in her eyes was gone.

"But you seemed to know," she persisted.

"Oh, maybe I detected a little accent. Stockholm, I would say."

Coolly she said, "But I don't have an accent." When he merely shrugged she continued, "I was there only as a child."

"In Sweden?"

"Stockholm, actually, but no one says I have an accent. I don't think I have an accent. What makes you say I do?"

27

Again he shrugged. "I don't know. I was there a few times. I guess I pick up on people's accents."

"That's a little more than *picking up*, I'd say." He had upset her, and she eyed him. "Maybe you have some kind of language gift . . . and maybe you don't."

He nodded. "Maybe I do not," he agreed, his tone conciliatory.

She had considered herself in charge of the conversation, until his assertion, and her anger seethed at conceding her place. But this was not play and should not be personal. Forcing the anger into submission, she queried pleasantly, "So, how many languages do you know?"

"Not many," he replied.

Finished with the beer, she held the bottle aloft and looked at the light through its neck. "I always do this," she said. "I love colored glass. I use glass in my sculptures. Do you like sculpture?"

He nodded.

She decided to push. "Can I see your work, the photography?"

He lifted his shoulders. "Sure, okay." Then he added, "And maybe I could see your work, too, if that would be okay."

"Sure, I'd like that. I always show what I've got and show it when I can."

He tried to neutralize the double entendre by smiling, but failed. He could not keep looking at her grinning mouth, but looking into the salacious, twinkling eyes would have been worse, so he looked at her hair and said nothing.

Pleasurably she waited just a moment longer and then blurted, "God, I hate sexless men. You're not sexless, are you?"

"I, um, think sometimes I am, actually."

She laughed aloud, sputtering, "Oh God, get out. Okay, well, I guess that's cool. All right, I'll talk to Martina, and she can bring you by sometime. Cool. See you."

It had always irritated him to have anyone turn away from him with a chuckle. He considered the behavior to be either insensitive or deliberately insulting. He was not certain which it was now, but could not resist thinking it was the latter. Then Martina was standing beside him, touching his arm. As she spoke the very vibrations of her voice seemed to quell his tremors.

"How about another sandwich, Mr. Osipov?"

He was not hungry, but he was ready to have her make as many sandwiches for him as she wanted, if only he could watch her make them, could stand beside her, listen to her, talk to her. He was not hungry, but that did not matter, for he would eat what he could and take the rest home. He did not need to have it at home to eat later, unless it was to have it there, knowing that she had made it. He was not hungry for sandwiches, he was hungry for her.

"I would love to have another sandwich. Will you make it for me?"

She took a moment to look into the placid blue eyes, then took his arm, pulled him to the sandwich table, and began to make the sandwich. She knew, of course, that his interest was not in food. Still, he was like a child as he stood watching her, his eyes fixed upon her. But he was not a child, he was a man, and she wondered if he had gotten enough of the lascivious Gretchin, whether she had annoyed him or enticed him. Men could be such a bundle of nonsense, she thought, such a package of foolishness. They were like sandwiches—you put them together, gave them a pat, and sliced them open, only to find there was nothing inside but what you had put there to begin with, simply meat and mayonnaise. Somehow, after all the preparation, you expected to be rewarded with magic, but you only ended up with food.

She did not make him one sandwich but three. And she did not put them on a plate, but wrapped them in waxed paper, put them in a paper bag, and placed them in the refrigerator, saying she knew he wasn't hungry and that he could take them with him when he left. Then she led him to the living room to meet Bradley Hopkins, her principal, who had just arrived. After introducing the two men she left them. They watched her walk away, then faced each other and shook hands.

The Russian smiled. "Hi. Bradley?"

"Yes, *Brad*," the other returned confidently. "Martina calls me Bradley, but I don't like it much. I like it shorter, it sounds more American." He thrust his clean-shaven chin forward, as if to emphasize this. Glad that he was the taller of the two men, he smiled radiantly and ran a hand over the top of his crewcut. "So," he said, "I guess it's *Stan*, then?"

"If you like, okay," replied the Russian, judging the man to be in his early forties. "But *Stanley* is fine, too. You are the principal at Martina's school?"

"Absolutely. I'm the guy."

"Do not tell me. You were in the military. I would guess the Air Force, a desk. I am guessing, so do not hate me, yes?"

"Man, that's sick," exclaimed the other, his eyes round. "Hey, you're pretty good. How'd you know that?"

Shifting his weight, the Russian put his hands into his pockets. He wanted to say that the stamp on the forehead had given it all away, but instead he replied, "It was only a guess. Maybe it was your voice or something else, I do not know. You seem to have something military about you. The motto is *Above All*, right?"

Beaming happily, "Yep, you got it. *Up, Up And Away*. Hey, you must study these things." And he grinned broadly, taking a moment to bask in the recognition. Then he said, "You're a photographer, sir, is that right? Not that your slouchy clothes gave it away." Here he laughed aloud.

The Russian nodded, his face blank. "Yes, Brad, I am a photographer."

Still jovial, the principal reached for Stanley's sleeve. "Say, come in here, let's look at the new TV. Who's going to win this game? I love football. There's something about it, like it belongs to us."

Another nod. "To Americans?"

"Yes, absolutely. I mean, I know every country's got its sports. But football and baseball—man, they're ours."

"What about NASCAR?"

"Oh yeah," returned the other as they approached the huge glowing screen. "Yeah, sure, NASCAR, unbelievable. I love cars. I've got a Vette. It's gorgeous, a great car. And the power, you should feel it, it's unbelievable. You just mash the gas, man, and the thing eats asphalt. Ah, unbelievable." He shook his head in amazement. "So many things are ours. What a great country. Don't you think?"

Wincing, Stanley replied, "Yes. Yes, it is.

CHAPTER 3

Although she had wished it to be different this year, Martina found the preholiday week to be even busier and more frustrating than usual. Thanks to the upcoming Christmas vacation the average attention span in her class seemed to hover just above zero. Some teachers gave up in their attempts to teach during the week leading up to the Christmas break and showed movies to their class instead. By Friday she too had given up. Indeed, she was showing a video when Stanley called to confirm their plans for the evening. They were to go to Gretchin's for dinner and to see her art. Although he had phoned a few times during the week, she had not seen him since Sunday's party.

"Are you happy, Ms. Jung?"

Standing like a sentry at the door of her classroom, Martina looked down into the brown eyes of the little girl. It was an odd query, and had caught her unaware. With no idea how to answer, she replied, "What makes you ask that, Jennifer?"

As the other students, nearly in a frenzy, left the classroom the girl stood calm. She did not know what had made her ask the question.

"Well, Jennifer, don't I look happy?"

The girl shrugged, her inquisitive expression constant.

Finally Martina said, "Yes, I am happy, of course I am happy."

The girl brightened, but persisted, "And will you be happy on Christmas, Ms. Jung?"

"Will you, Jennifer?"

"I'm always happy on Christmas."

"I will be visiting my sisters, and that will make me happy. What are you going to do for Christmas, Jennifer?"

The girl smiled. "I have a dog and I'm going to spend it with him. I love him *so* much, Ms. Jung. He's, like, beautiful, and he loves me."

"That's wonderful, good. And he's loyal too, no doubt. Loyalty's just as important as love, knowing he'll stick with you, and everything."

"Oh, he's *way* loyal."

"Well, I'm going to close up now, Jennifer. So, have a good holiday and I'll see you in the new year." And as the brown eyes continued to stare up at her, she added, "And thanks for asking, it was nice of you. Merry Christmas, Jennifer."

"Merry Christmas, Ms. Jung."

It was later, after he had picked her up and they were driving into the city, that she thought again of the little girl and her question. It was not often that a student asked a question that was deep enough to haunt you. It was phenomenal when it did happen, and you had no response except to take it all with you—yes, take the question with you, there in the deepest part of you, but also in your memory.

"I was asked today," she said as Broad Street looked especially cold to her through the glass, "by one of my students, an intelligent little girl, if I was happy. It was remarkable."

"Yes? And what did you answer?"

She was silent for a moment, but then, watching him as he drove, "What would you have answered?"

"I do not know. I suppose you have to lie a little more to children. But still, I would not know what to say. It is a strange question. Everybody asks it, and nobody knows the answer. I do not know if I am happy. Who would know the answer to such a question?"

And now he seemed terribly sensitive, so that she forced her gaze away from him to look at the cold surfaces of the city. She reminded herself that the enemy was never sensitive, that it was a mistake to think he could be, and that this enemy was no exception to the rule. When they looked for a parking spot on 2nd Street and he complained that the city parking was ludicrous she said sarcastically that she supposed the parking was really good in Moscow.

"Ah, you are brutal," he laughed, backing them into a space. "No, of course it is not. You are right, it is terrible, just like here."

As they walked she took his arm and said that it was chilly but must be chillier in Moscow. She pulled him closer, and they laughed as they walked. It felt good to be out with him, she thought, although the prospect of spending the evening with him at Gretchin's disturbed her. Perhaps too often she had seen Gretchin in action.

Suddenly, after they had turned a corner, she remarked how Gretchin was quite an artsy girl and that she doubted if such a person could ever live in the suburbs. She said she knew Gretchin, that she was really just a city rat at heart, an artsy, slinky city rat. But when he did not respond to this she regretted saying it. She should keep more control of her emotions, keep jealousy completely out of it. This was her work—the man, the relationship, the information—all of it, and she must never allow the work to be compromised.

Then they were quiet and close as they walked through the cold. When they turned onto a tiny cobblestone street they swayed together over the uneven blocks. The thought of Gretchin sporting her cleavage all evening had made her choose heels instead of more comfortable and warmer flats, but as the cobblestones made her wobble and squeeze his arm she felt foolish and cursed herself for pitting heels against cleavage, and that of a younger woman. But then, she checked herself, for again, this was work and both she and Gretchin were after the same cold thing.

"She's just up here," she said, stepping onto the sidewalk.

At a wrought iron-grated white door at sidewalk level they stopped for her to ring the bell. The entrance was well lit and a little carved wooden sign presented gold lettering that said 'Gretchin's Place.'

"The ginkos along here are awful," she observed, "but it looks like somebody's swept up. The fruit is horrible, it smells for months, unless there's a heavy snow. I don't know why the city puts them in."

"They are supposed to thrive in the city and the shade is good."

She nodded, hugging herself with both arms, but then smiled as the door opened.

"The colleague and the photographer." Gretchin said. "Come in, come in."

Pushing a handful of hair behind an ear, she stepped aside for them and then closed the door. After putting their coats on wooden hangers on a clothes tree, she led them through an alcove and into an oversized living room. A console CD player by a brick wall emitted the low sounds of jazzy Bach piano.

"This is very nice," Stanley remarked. "Your ceilings are so high."

"Yeah, but no closets, which is why I have to use a tree. But I like it. It used to be a warehouse of some kind. I use this as a living room. The whole building's kind of utilitarian. I have the two bottom floors. It's a good space for my stuff."

He felt that he must say something, so he remarked that the room was a cube. Laughing, she said that it was close, but missed it by a foot. Martina interjected that he had to see Gretchin's second-floor studio.

"Yeah, we'll take a tour later," Gretchin piped. "Hope you're hungry, I've got a couple pizzas going. Take a look around, I have some things on the walls. Martina, I could use your help. We can eat in here, I think. Stanley, how about a beer?"

"Um, water's okay for me."

The aqua eyes sparkled mischievously. "Oh, come on. Water. What are you, green?"

He gave a faint shrug. "Okay, maybe a soda, if you have one."

She raised her hands. "I give up. He wants the hard stuff."

With his eyes he followed the two women until they disappeared into the kitchen. Then instantly he recalled their images as if he had filmed them. The art teacher, herself so much a reptile as to be taken for a breathing version of the dragon on her neck, had padded in her bare feet across the worn oriental rug as if it was a tapestry of the sexual history of the species, while the English teacher, sensuous as a reptile, yes, but also dignified as an old-world monarch, had walked with simple assurance across the same rug. Only Europeans, he knew, could do that.

Wondering why he had never moved from photography to film, he turned his attention to the art that decorated the spacious room. Paintings, drawings, and photographs, framed eclectically, had been hung at three levels upon two walls. He sighed deeply, for he had always found in art, at least true art, the strange quality of consolation, as if the artist's original inspiration resided still in the created thing, ever ready to absolve and grant peace. It didn't have to be great art or even what people said was great art, but it did have to be true art. Challenged once to define true art, he had declined to make an attempt, sensing the imminence of failure. He had replied only that all the true things were elusive to definition, requiring only belief to release their power.

"What do you think?" Gretchin asked, suddenly beside him. Before he could reply, she added, in a colder tone, "Don't take my question seriously. I didn't really ask. I can't stand criticism, positive or negative."

He blinked and chuckled. "You have warned me."

"I have."

"How about praise? I like your things."

"That I can take. Give me more, mister photographer. Here's your sody pop—hope you're not driving."

He tasted the drink, then continued soberly, "I met a guard a number of years ago, a security guard in a museum in Europe. I was just there one day, and we started talking. I had been looking at a collection of modern paintings, and he had been watching me, I think. Just for no reason, I asked him how he fought the boredom of guarding things in silence day after day. He chuckled and said his greatest weapon was amusement. He said he was especially entertained by watching people show the same emotions before both the real and fake versions of a piece of art. Occasionally, when they were short on security for an exhibition, the curators, this guard said, would substitute fakes for valuable pieces. They only did this with a few pieces, but every time, it worked. Everyone, he said, including the museum's elite patrons, would fawn over the fake and the genuine just the same. He said it kept him awake. He would sit on his stool in his corner and laugh inside."

"I imagine he would," she said, pushing hair behind an ear.

He sipped the Coke. "So, I asked him why he laughed."

"And?"

"He said because he knew the truth that all art was fake. When I suggested that maybe being bored and observing a few incidents had made him cynical and that people usually just came to museums to find refreshment in beauty, he replied that I was like all the rest, that there was no such thing as beauty, and that I appreciated it only because I had learned life that way."

"Sounds like he had a lot bottled up."

"Oh, he did, yes. I told him that I believed there was such a thing as beauty and that I had experienced its joys many times."

"Don't tell me, you got a snicker from him."

"Yes, I think I did," he chuckled. "He said he knew that artists were just people who would do anything to get out of work, that they would cut a piece of marble, chop at it a bit, call it something odd, and then market it. He said he knew there was nothing in the art itself worth looking at and that those of us who said there was something to see were simply being fooled by our ambitions and our fears."

She sighed. "And you said what?"

"I told him I saw art more as a voice than a product and that it needed to be first acknowledged and then carefully listened to before it could speak."

"He must've barfed at that."

"Yes, exactly," he laughed. "He told me I was wasting my time waiting for art to speak, that I might as well wait for God to speak. Then he frowned, then laughed, then went back to his stool and sat and watched me, yes."

She did not care for serious anecdotes, nor for sobriety. Suddenly she grabbed the glass from him, took a quick drink from it, and pushed it back into his hand. "You know something?" she said impatiently. "Some guys just need a good woman to warm them up and make them believe again. By the way, you need some liquor in that."

He thought she looked like a gypsy as she walked away, and then he heard their voices from the kitchen and turned to look at more of the art. "Just stay busy," Martina called to him, "it'll be ready soon." But as he looked at the pictures, not seeing or thinking about their surfaces, their frames or any of it, he thought again of the fur and the blood and the snowflakes. Some of it had gone, but most of it, he knew, would be with him forever, and all of that would always be as real as it had been that day.

"Spoons?" queried Martina as the two women prepared the dinner.

Reaching for a mitt, Gretchin wrinkled her nose. "Why not? We might have coffee." Then, in a whisper, "Well, this one's interesting. God, what a gloomy man."

41

After rolling up three sets of utensils in napkins, Martina remarked, "You certainly seem interested."

"What do you mean?"

"Never mind."

"He is a photographer, for God's sake, what do you expect from me? Photographers and artists are visually stimulated people. We can't help it."

"*It?*"

Peeking into the oven, Gretchin replied, still in a whisper, but annoyed, "I don't know, Martina. You fill in the blank."

"Oh, I have, don't worry. But you're not the only visually stimulated people, right?"

Wrinkling her nose again, the other only said, in a normal tone, "The pizza's ready. I'm going to keep it on the stone, it'll stay really hot. I love these things. Let's take everything in."

He turned to watch as they put a towel and the hot stone on the coffee table. He thought of Moscow, the family gatherings. He marveled that those times were more real to him now than when he lived them. Even the people seemed more real to him now than when he knew them and talked with them. But perhaps he had just grown older and was beginning to prefer his memories over reality.

"Gretchin," he said, "you must have a hundred pieces in here. It is impressive, it is an exhibit."

Tasting a drip of tomato sauce, she smiled up at him. "But some of them are really old. Some go back to college."

"It is remarkable," he observed, taking a seat beside her on the couch and adjusting a cushion, "how well the odors of turpentine and pizza mix."

"They're friends," she laughed.

"But is that right?" he asked. "Is the word *odor* the right word I want?"

Martina, from the stuffed chair she had chosen opposite to them, suggested, "Maybe *odor of turpentine* and *aroma of pizza* would work."

He was jubilant and said he would try to remember it. She replied that she doubted if he could forget it, considering his powers of language, for it was obvious that he was nearly a linguist. But she was the English teacher, he said, so he would take his cue from her. And perhaps Maggie could teach him history, he added, genuinely amused, and Gretchin could teach him art. Annoyed by this last suggestion, Martina reached for the bottle and offered him more soda.

"But how would you say in good English," he asked, "more like literature, that *turpentine is so really strong*?"

"Maybe you could say, *it has a pungent odor*," she answered. "My father would always clean the paint brushes with it, until he couldn't get it anymore, during the war, or paint, for that matter."

Gretchin, folding a slice of the pizza, said, "That would've been gum turp. They rectify it for art. Otherwise, a painting will crack if it's used in the paint."

Martina smiled placidly. She wondered whether a love affair would happen between Gretchin and this subject of theirs. Her eyes rested upon the blank Russian face of Stanley Osipov. Would he prefer sleeping with Gretchin or herself? Impulsively she asked, "What are you thinking right now, Mr. Osipov? Tell us."

Momentarily he replied, "I am not certain. Perhaps, I am thinking about America. And what are *you* thinking right now, Ms. Jung? You have to say."

"I am not certain, either," she returned coolly. "Perhaps, Russia."

"So, Martina," blurted Gretchin, "the holidays, is it the same thing for you this year?"

A sigh. "Yes, I'm afraid so. I'm off to Vermont tomorrow, thank you. And I won't be looking back."

The other scratched her neck delicately just above the dragon. "You'll be going to the farm?"

An affirmative nod.

"But why?"

"Why what?"

"Why always the farm? Why not get together in the city or have everyone come here?"

"We like it there. It's peaceful and beautiful."

Gretchin shrugged. "You've never come across that way to me. I mean, you know, *farm* and all that."

"And how have I come across to you, then, Gretchin?"

"I don't know. Maybe a little *society,* I guess. I don't know, Martina. But not *farm.*"

Quelling her irritation, Martina offered icily, "Well, it's nice there, very nice. It's quiet, and I can think. We could get together somewhere else, but the farm always works for us. It brings back a lot of memories, helps us to keep things together. I'm looking forward to it."

Taking his eyes from Martina's hair, Stanley offered, "But I think you would make a good farmer."

Gretchin cocked her head unhappily, for she could not picture Martina as anything but a standup doll. "Uh, I think you're a little nuts there, bud."

"Well," he returned, "maybe on a little farm."

She looked at Martina. "And you'll be doing *family* too," she cooed. "That's really cute."

"I don't see my sisters much, so it will be good. Do you see your mother very often, Stanley?"

He shrugged. "No, only one time a year. And if I have the money, two times."

With a sniff of indifference, Gretchin queried, "And will you be going alone, Martina?"

Nearly choking from incredulity, Martina took a moment to control her composure. All of her wanted to say it plainly that she considered the other not only a wretched slut but a classless wench. And she would have loved to add that she considered her a social saboteur of the first order. Instead, her eyes upon Stanley's inquisitive gaze, she replied that of course she would be going alone, that she always did.

CHAPTER 4

On the day before New Year's Eve Martina returned from Vermont. As she had done every year since the reunions at the farm began, she determined to return refreshed and ready to begin the new year. For the work at school, of course, the beginning of a new calendar year presented an opportunity for her to launch her class a second time. For the other work, the work she had come to value, perhaps love, above all the enterprises she had ever undertaken, such a beginning presented an opportunity to reenter the pit and face the beast with a fresh scent of its blood.

It had been a joyful Christmas at the farm. Sophia had been happy, and Milla and Klaus had been happy. They had all opened gifts in the early morning and drunk German beer with the Christmas dinner. In the afternoon they had taken a sleigh ride at a nearby horse farm to commemorate the glorious last ride of their youth near Berlin. And sitting before the log fire in the evenings, they had brought out their memories one by one and tendered their respects to the people who had decorated their lives in Germany. Of course, the final memory to be honored had been, as every year, that of their escape, how Father had awakened them in the middle of the night and told them to be quiet and to bring nothing but their clothes; how they had obeyed without question, connecting it all to Mother's death; how the drive had been long and gloomy, with stops only to relieve themselves in the snow while Father poured fuel into the tank from cans and glass jugs; how, later, they had learned that it had cost absolutely everything to get them out, and that even then, Father had been successful only because he had known the right people.

"Oh, Maggie," she said, pulling a chair from the kitchen table, "I wish you had come."

With a few strokes she brushed her hair out and then leaned with satisfaction against the back of the chair, luxuriously working her toes to the end of her softest slippers. She looked at the green eyes, the ivory skin, the Presley hair. It was so very, very good to be home. Life was like that, it sometimes gave you itself so sweetly in giving you the past, the present, and an apparent future. It gave you family to visit, memories to cherish, and friends to come home to. You wondered how it could give you more.

"You always come back in this ethereal mood," returned Maggie, unimpressed. "Vermont is not heaven, dear, it's just the woods."

"It was so beautiful."

"You always say that," Maggie replied, her eyes following the red stripes of her friend's robe until they touched the floor. "You don't seem to get it, Vermont in the winter is not a place I want to be. Philadelphia is cold enough for me, thank you." She gave a shudder, to illustrate her contempt for the cold, and got up.

"You're just a beach bum."

"I'm a cat," corrected Maggie, placing two sets of plates and egg cups on the table. Checking the timer, she said, "Reach us a couple of spoons and cups for tea."

"And not a snow leopard, huh?"

"No."

"But you have no idea how beautiful it was, how wonderful it could be if you would only go with me one time."

"I guess I don't."

"But you actually missed a sleigh ride."

"No, thank you."

"Christmas beside a log fire is poignant."

"I liked it here. And I kept the heat up, I can tell you. It was wonderful. I watched TV. You know, that's a great screen. I would never have dreamed a television could be that big and that bright and clear. Besides, I told you, I know what it means to you to get away. If I had gone, you wouldn't have gotten away. It wouldn't have been just family."

"Well," said Martina, still rapturous, pulling her chair up to the table and smoothing the white cloth beside the plate, "I missed you and I wish you had come. Sophia, Milla and Klaus said to say hi. And they sent you a gift."

"I told you to tell them."

"They wouldn't listen."

Maggie groaned audibly. Then, as if in one motion, she lifted the egg pot from the stove top, drained its hot water, filled it with cold from the tap, set it upon the table tile between them, and sat down. Then, as if forfeiting a minor point in the game, she offered, "I'll write them."

"That would be good, and say something about Christmas."

"I will, dear."

Both women knew the conversation had run its course, that it had been nonsensical but also necessary. For although they no longer needed to affirm their relationship, they always seemed to need to enjoy it. Verbally reaching and touching was as necessary as the meals they ate together. When they had opened their eggs and tasted their tea, they settled into their usual niche of peace.

"Did that thing come from Amazon?" queried Martina.

"It's on your dresser, dear."

"Did anybody call?"

"Stanley."

Squinting predatorily, Martina said softly, "Good, that's what we want. Did he say anything?"

"No, he just breathed into the phone, dear."

"You know what I mean."

"No, nothing significant."

"Anybody else?"

Maggie sniffed. "Richard."

"Good grief, give us some time, please."

"He just wanted to know if the bait had been taken."

Martina lifted her eyes. "Well, as we all know, I'm the bait. And no, he hasn't taken me yet."

"I don't think he meant that."

Martina shrugged, scooping deliberately at the egg with her spoon. "I know. But he's always so pushy. He annoys me."

"You sound exasperated, dear."

"Yeah, a little bit. I mean, this guy is in my hand. And I don't need Richard telling me to screw the guy over Christmas. I mean, please, I can't even visit my sisters, for God's sake." She shook her head and drove the spoon through the bottom of the egg.

Maggie shifted in her chair. "I wouldn't get so upset."

"Well, Richard knows I go away at Christmas. Every year. It's not sporadic, it's every year. But he has to call, as if I shouldn't be away, or like, if he pushes hard enough I'll come back and get to work. That's an attitude. He shouldn't treat us that way."

"We're just advisors. Everybody in the group is."

"I know that, Maggie, okay?"

"You don't need to get testy dear. There's nothing you can do about it. It's the way Richard is."

"But he doesn't need to sport his superiority all the time. Or his discipline, like he's disciplined and we're not."

"So, you don't think they're all anxious? You think it's just Richard?"

A nod, and then, "I am convinced, though—Mr. Osipov is the real deal. They were dead-on right about that." She touched her lips lightly with her napkin. "I'll call Richard."

"Good idea, dear."

"Yeah," Martina uttered dejectedly. "Merry Christmas."

Maggie looked across at the blond hair, the gray eyes. "You mean," she said, "Happy New Year."

"You have that *look*, Maggie. What?"

Another sniff. "You know, Martina," she said in a softer tone, "you have much to be thankful for."

Wryly, "What is that supposed to mean?"

The gaze of the green eyes dropped, then lifted. "It means, dear, that you are really quite beautiful."

"So are you, and you know it. So what?"

Maggie sighed. "Most women don't look like you do at sixty-eight, and they're not as healthy as you are, and they're not as clear thinking as you are, and they're not as free as you are."

"A four-point sermon?"

Smiling patiently, "You're sixty-eight, dear."

"What does my age have to do with it?"

"With what?"

"Your sermon, I suppose, or our being attractive, I don't know. Get on with it, say it."

The green eyes met the gray eyes. "You're almost seventy. You might look like you're fifty, but you're not. Your beauty is going to decline, dear, sometime. In ten years, fifteen, but it is going to decline."

Annoyed, Martina lifted her cup, took a sip from it, and said, "So is yours."

The other nodded. "I know. God, how I know. I feel old now."

Martina put the cup down, no longer annoyed. She wondered why life had such a penchant for leading her into absurd situations. Here she was, arguing with the dearest person in her life, one of the few people who truly cared about her, someone who had only wanted to tender a concerned warning. Then she lifted the cup again and said, "Well, you look pretty good now, Maggie, so don't worry about it. I see the way men walk past you. They look, they turn, or something, but they can't seem to pass you in neutrality. You're sixty-three and they still look, and the way they look would flatter *any* woman. You're beautiful *and* seductive, so why the sermon?"

Maggie blinked, then replied, "I don't really know. It was just something I think I needed to say." She sipped her tea. "So, you are going to call Richard?"

"Yes. Yes, of course."

"And Stanley?"

"Oh, yes," Martina replied, a note of cunning in her voice. "We must call Stanley, we must call Mr. Osipov." Then she pushed her chair back and stood. "But right now I'm going to have a long, Sunday afternoon bath in herbal water."

"Oh, yes?"

"For my health and beauty."

"Yes."

In the early evening, with supper finished and the dishwasher humming, they carried the tray of tea and cookies to the front room and sat. As Maggie unfolded the Sunday newspaper and spread its sections like a huge hand of playing cards over the coffee table, Martina observed the ritual in silence. One of the great pleasures they shared together was watching each other's mundane actions, as if observing something important, timeless.

Satisfied with the spacing of the sections, Maggie brought the silence to an end. "You look a little strange, dear. You're not doing the game again, are you?"

"No."

"Most sighted people would imagine blindness to be a terrible world to live in, and an ugly world. Some people who have become blind have described it as a sort of ugly, yellow-gray darkness."

"So I've heard."

"Yet, you make a game of it."

"And the harm? It's an escape."

"So you've said," Maggie replied with a sigh. She did not want to hear again how Martina had started the game at home as a young girl and continued to play it into adulthood, how at first she had needed to close her eyes to play it but soon could play it with her eyes open, even while looking into someone's face.

"Vision," said Martina, reaching for the pot of steeping tea, "is only one of the senses. It doesn't aid in the appreciation of an aroma, for instance."

"You've made the point before, dear."

A shrug of unconcern. "It's just a game."

In turn, each took a saucer and cup and poured tea from the old English pot. An unconditional love for drinking English breakfast tea from bone china tea sets was something they knew they would share forever.

"Shall I go ahead?" Martina queried, fixing her gaze upon her friend's fingers as they slid down the edge of a page of newsprint.

The green eyes flickered with irritation. "Now?"

"I was thinking that."

"Can't we have our tea and look at the paper?" Carefully she extracted the fashion section and opened it.

"Of course. Just read."

The green eyes closed. "It wouldn't be the same," she acquiesced. "Go ahead, call him. My antennae are up."

Martina lifted the phone, selected the number, momentarily said, "Yes, Richard? This is Martina," and then rolled her eyes at his predictable pause. Through experience, she had come to the conclusion that he could not speak to her without, at least initially, pausing for effect.

"How was your trip?" he asked.

"Oh, very nice, refreshing, cold. It was good to see the family."

Another pause, then, "That's good. I'm glad you enjoyed yourself. Everyone well?"

"Yes, thank you."

"One question, what about Osipov?"

"I thought you would never ask," she said facetiously.

Icily, "But I *am* asking, Martina."

What an asshole, she muttered to herself. God, he could irritate her, just in the way he could say things, just like this. But then she answered calmly, "I think he's real, I think we've got one."

His tone was matter-of-fact. "That's good. We thought so. Okay, well, you know the routine. Get to know him, whatever it takes, and then find out. And keep close to your team. I think you should see them and talk things through. Make a good plan, but keep it loose and natural, everything as usual. You know what you're doing. Any problems, call me. And keep me posted, I don't have a crystal ball."

"Surely." Then, hearing the connection die, she close the phone and put it down.

"It's just a phone, dear," Maggie said, "not something dirty."

The gray eyes became slits. "That depends," she replied, "upon the voice that fouls it. We don't really like each other."

"We know that, dear, we all know that."

"Everything he says is an insult, or do I imagine it?"

"You're not imagining it, dear." She turned a page and gave the section a shake. "So, what's next?"

Reaching for the teapot, "He said to get the team together."

"He always believes you, doesn't he? I mean, when you say you think someone *is* or *isn't*, he never seems to question your judgment. He doesn't ask you how you know."

"I wish the others had his faith."

"That might not be the best word, dear, not with Richard, not *faith*."

An affirming nod. "Anyway, why don't you email them? Here's fine. I think it's our turn. I hope it is, I don't want to go out."

"I will do that, dear, I will, but now, let's have tea—just properly, *tea*."

"Shall I call Mr. Osipov now?"

"Not now, dear. Just tea."

Later, after she had wiped the last of the cold cream from her face, Martina quietly closed her bedroom door, then made her last call of the day.

"Stanley?"

"Hi, Martina. Welcome back."

"Thank you, Stanley, and Merry Christmas, if you do that."

"I do it," he laughed. "I wish for you a Merry Christmas, and I wish for you a Happy New Year."

Momentarily, "Thank you."

"How have you been doing? How was your trip?"

"I had a good time, it was a very pleasant trip."

"Your family?"

"Fine, thanks."

"You will have to tell me about Vermont. I was reading about it, and it seems to be like Russia, I think. This is exaggeration, but maybe a little bit like Russia."

"It's pretty."

"It is pretty in Russia also, but only in certain parts. You will have to tell me about your visit with your family."

As she looked at her face in the dresser mirror she blinked, for the face seemed like that of a clown who had just removed the paint after the evening's show. A moment later she replied, "I'd love to tell you about it."

"It is good to hear your voice. It seems like you have been gone a long time."

"Yes, well, and now I'm back, and tomorrow's New Year's Eve." When he said nothing to this, she said, "So, do you celebrate, or . . . or not?"

"Not really," he began, but then, "but I am thinking, would you like to come out with me?"

"Celebrate?"

"Yes, of course, celebrate."

"That would be very nice, I would love to go."

"I will come to your house to pick you up at about six?"

"Six would be fine, sure."

"Do I dress up?"

Smiling to herself, she answered, "Oh, I think casual would be fine. We don't have to make a big thing of it. We can just see what's going on down in the city, or whatever."

"Good, that is very good."

Then she said good night and closed the phone, her eyes upon the clown's face in the mirror.

Just before six the next day, she sat at the dresser and brushed her hair. The bone-handled brush had been her mother's. Carefully she laid the heirloom down and looked at it. She loved to hold it, for always it seemed warm from the hand of her mother, and inviting, as if it wished to be held and used by someone of the next generation. It had not come with them out of Germany, but by way of a friend who had snatched it from the house after their escape and sent it to them in America. Everyone had wanted her to have it, so she took it and kept and held it in her hand every day. But now it was six o'clock, so she laid it down, pushed it away with her fingertips, and got up.

Then the bell rang and she went down and opened the door and pulled him in quickly from the cold. For a moment, he just stood and looked at her, a wrapped gift in his hand. When she offered to take his coat he held the gift out to her, muttering stupidly that it was chocolates, but then corrected himself, calling it just a gift. They laughed about her not needing to guess after that, and she felt again the melancholy of his personality. When she left to get her coat she sensed that he was looking at her. Returning with the gift she had for him, she noted that his eyes were not upon the gift, but upon her hair.

"I had wanted to give you this for Christmas," she apologized, "but it didn't arrive in time."

He held the package as a child would, touching its bow. He asked if he should guess what it was. When she shook her head he shook his too, insisting that she open hers first. She did and remarked that they were expensive and looked to be delicious. Then she watched as he opened his, watched him closely, for he was her work, her assignment, and she always kept the crosshairs centered upon the target. Carefully he removed the wrapping from the gift, reading aloud the DVD's title *The Guns of August.* She said it was a kind of consolation for his looking so disappointed in the store that day.

"I will not invite you to watch it with me," he promised.

Then she smiled, both to him and to herself, for all was going as it should.

CHAPTER 5

When they left she took his arm. It was good to feel him close to her again. She recalled their walk along the cold city sidewalks on their way to Gretchin's. She was glad not to have to compete with a younger woman for his attention this evening. She was also glad to find not only that he had left the car's engine running for warmth but that he had cleaned its interior. Luxuriously she stretched her legs as they drove away.

He saw this and asked, "Do you like being driven?"

"I do," she admitted, "Actually, I do very much. Why?"

"Some women these days would find it to be sort of—"

"Custodially romantic?"

"Yes," he laughed. "That must be correct. I would not have thought of it. I did not know it."

"Maybe I coined it."

"*Coined*, I do not know this either."

"*To coin* is *to invent*, sort of," she shot back, but then checked her impatience.

"And the other term?"

"*Custodial* means, like, *supervisory*, *taking care of*. *Romantic* you know, I'm sure. It doesn't matter, my term would not be happily received *these days*, as you say."

"And what about you, I am asking."

"I'm a mix of old school and new school, I guess. I insist on freedom, but I leave the hormones alone. I believe that testosterone isn't estrogen and that one screws with nature at one's own hazard. Is that clear, or maybe that's not clear. Did I answer your question?"

"Well, so, you are not angry if the man is usually driving the car, yes?"

Softly she answered, "Yes. I mean, no, it doesn't make me angry."

Occasionally she turned to watch him as he drove, his eyes as he navigated through the traffic. No, she did not mind being driven, and she watched through the cold car glass as the world passed away with no power to touch her. But this man had the power to touch her, to reach the inner part of her with his words, his ways. His simplest questions somehow disturbed her, for they reached her, and she had intend not to allow herself to be reached.

"How is Maggie," he queried. "I did not see her."

Momentarily, "She is out for the evening with a friend."

"You are close to Maggie, it is easy to see this."

"Yes, very close."

"You are like sisters."

"Yes."

"But more."

"Yes."

"What is the term—*same spirits*?"

"*Kindred spirits*."

"Yes. It is easy to see."

"Yes, we are very close. And how about you, do you have any kindred spirits?"

"No," he answered, glancing at her. "There is no one who is like that for me." Grinning, he added, "And we are going to weep, yes?"

Ignoring this last statement, she queried, "So, what would you say appeals to you in a film about war, why do you watch them?"

Bringing them to a red light, he looked up through the windshield to watch for the green. "I am uncertain," he said, "how to answer."

"Would you say the weaponry interests you, or something else?"

The light turned green, and then they were moving.

"That is a good answer," he replied. "Most men like gadgets, and weapons are gadgets, security gadgets. See, it is my term, I have *coined* it, what do you think, is it possible," he asked, laughing, "have I done this? It is ridiculous," and he laughed again.

She could only think of the vast devastation, the destruction wreaked by man through his weaponry, his security gadgets. She wanted to ignore him, but knew she must not. She wanted to look out through the window, find some object of life, some living organism, and just look at it. Instead, she merely agreed, with as much enthusiasm as she could manufacture, that perhaps he had indeed coined the term.

"But also," he continued, becoming serious, "I think I watch war movies to see people believing in things. You have to believe in so much when you go to war—honor, family, country—so many things. You know, the point in the movie you gave me was that war wastes human life. But how can a faithful sacrifice ever be a waste?"

"When it's for a stupid cause."

"Yes, I know. But I am not certain that the cause matters very much."

"The morality of any war is in its cause, isn't it?"

"Yes, but I think there are more important things than morality."

"That's ridiculous."

He nodded. "Perhaps."

"And naive," she added, annoyed.

"Yes, perhaps."

"And dangerous."

He laughed. "Yes, perhaps it is dangerous."

Then they rode for a few moments in silence. Knowing he wanted to look at her, she reached for her purse, checked her phone for missed calls, and then shut it down completely.

"Expecting a call?" he asked.

"Not really. Just shutting it off."

He grinned. "They will keep calling, you cannot stop them."

"Probably not, but I tend to resist inevitability."

Repositioning his hand on the wheel, he said, "You seem to be good with electronics."

"I fight it, actually," she returned. "I thought everything was fine with regular telephones. When they came out with cell phones I wondered why anyone would ever want to carry the thing around. But everything seemed to change and become electronic. I resisted, but then I went peaceably, like everyone else."

"Now you are a geek, yes?"

"Not quite, I'm afraid."

"I went peaceably, too," he laughed. "I have a cell phone now, and a laptop, and a digital camera."

"The camera must have been a stretch."

"I admit it." Then he looked to see if she would smile. "Everything is digital now. I am used to it. It is all part of the system, yes?"

"Not afraid of Big Brother?"

He chuckled, but then replied soberly, "Afraid? I am afraid of everything. But you are not afraid of very much, yes?"

She looked at him, but did not answer.

At length he said, "I admire strong women."

"Yes?" she replied cautiously.

"And I admire also honest women."

"What do you call honesty—being candid?"

"More. It is more than that. Honesty is more like being true. It is a good definition, yes?"

After a moment she asked, "So, do you consider yourself to be true?"

He shook his head, but did not look at her.

Again she was at a place where she wanted to ignore him, or wanted him just to stop talking. She said nothing, but looked out her window. It was aggravating, she thought, that the very glass through which she looked was not as transparent as this man. But of course, her complaint was with herself, for how could she have wished for more than transparency? You wish for transparency in a target with a thick mask, but in one with a thin mask, or worse, with no mask at all, transparency is a dangerous thing, for seeing into the heart of the target makes it difficult, if not impossible for the shooter to pull the trigger.

"You are quiet," he observed.

"Yes," she whispered, closing her eyes.

"You are thinking?" he asked.

"Just playing a game."

"It is not a game for two?"

"No," she replied, her eyes still closed. "It's not really a game, it's just something I do."

They left the car in a parking garage near to city hall and walked west on Walnut Street.

At a small restaurant that looked appealing to them, they stepped inside to see if they could get a table. A woman in a festive black dress greeted them and then led them to a small table not far from the bar. She said they were lucky to find anything on New Year's Eve without a reservation.

Pulling her chair in, Martina said discreetly to Stanley, who hung their coats on a tree beside the table, "This is nice, this will be nice, perfect."

He took his seat, and after assessing their proximity to the bar, said that he could not be happier. The loaded coat tree, which had been oddly placed just beside the table, formed a barrier between them and the crowded bar. They were also situated between two stanchions and might as well have been in a corner.

She watched him as he made himself comfortable, as he lifted his menu, as he assessed again their privacy. She watched his eyes as he followed the menu items, and she was still watching when suddenly he looked at her and then marginally moved the tiny lamp.

"Your eyes, they are shining," he observed playfully. "What do we get tonight? What do you want to get?"

"I am not certain," she answered, feeling strangely unsure of herself. Usually life met her directly, presented itself simply as a puzzle, and required little more from her than an exercise of logic and patience. But sometimes it met her obliquely, presented itself more like a wraith, and required no logic or patience at all from her but a kind of relaxation. Finally she asked, "What are you going to have?"

They ordered steak and wine and then seemed to settle into a kind of euphoria of relaxation. By the time their salads arrived they had spoken only of trivial things.

"I do want us to have a good time," she said to him suddenly. And she could see that he was satisfied with the way things were going—satisfied with her, with himself. She wanted him to be pleased with all that was around him, for only then would he speak like a drunken man and tell her his deepest truths.

"It is what I wish for," he returned.

Almost mechanically she lifted her glass and tasted her wine. From beyond the coat tree, the sounds of merriment and cheer were beginning to come to life for the evening. Although it was still early, it felt good to know that the sentries of the holiday were on guard. She wanted to close her eyes and pretend to be blind and disengage from her responsibilities. When she began to wish that nothing mattered as much as it really did she checked herself, brought herself back.

And then he said, "You don't wear makeup, do you?"

She looked at him curiously. "And who is asking, the photographer or the man?"

"Photographers get away with asking questions that men cannot ask."

"I imagine they do," she returned. "Is that your answer?"

He shook his head. "No," he replied. "No, that is not my answer. I am not asking as a photographer."

After a moment she said, "I wear a little."

"You look very, very nice."

Smiling, "Thank you." And then, "Do you usually ask women about their makeup?"

"It was a stupid question, I am sorry. I think I will not ask it again this year."

She chuckled, lifting her glass to her lips. She could not decide what to call the blue in his eyes. "Let me ask *you* something, then. Why did you say no when I asked if you considered yourself to be true?"

When two men at the bar began to sing a premature *auld lang syne* she looked into his blue Russian eyes and saw that he was glad for the distraction of the singing, that at least for the present, he would not have to answer her question. But she did not care, for she had waited before, with others, and could wait now. Besides, being forced to wait for an answer always made collecting the information a little sweeter. No one else had joined in the singing, and soon the splendid duet came to a poignant close. Then she simply looked at him, her inquisitive gaze fixed upon him.

"Oh, yes," he responded, "your question, you would like an answer given."

"Well, maybe I shouldn't have asked it," she offered.

"No, no, that is fine. The question was good."

"So, what did you mean?"

He took a moment before responding. "I meant—I mean now—that I have not told you everything."

"I think that makes sense," she shrugged. "I haven't told you everything, either, I'm sure. And we haven't known each other that long. Often people don't tell each other things until much later, anyway."

"Yes, that must be true. But I am not sure that works right now—at least, not for me."

She was very pleased now, for he was obviously disturbed. Sensing his anxiety, she sniffed, as a wolf would sniff. Exhaling slowly, pleasurably, she scrutinized him. She could not believe that she had not been authorized to record him. Here she was, about to pull the world from his mouth, but she could not record him. Cursing to herself, she leaned closer to him and in a low voice said, "But I think you've told me quite a lot about yourself. What else would you like to tell me?"

Looking at her hair and eventually into her eyes, he lowered his voice as she had done and replied, "I worked for many years as a photographer for the Russian government. I was assigned to the KGB."

She forced a look of shocked surprise and then said, "I'm listening, Stanley." Then she watched with relish as he swallowed nervously, looked down at his coffee and then back at her. He was her prey. She had him. These moments, she had found, were nearly orgasmic.

"The details are not important, I think, but the KGB during the cold war, which was when I worked for them, was serious in its intent, if you know my meaning."

She nodded.

Sighing heavily, he continued, "Sometimes, you know, I provided information—photographs—of people suspected by KGB to be criminals in some way. I was assigned to take photographs as proof or whatever, I am not sure, but sometimes, I suppose if they were satisfied, they then went and destroyed the people."

"You mean, destroy their reputations?"

He swallowed again. "Well, I do not know. Sometimes, maybe. But sometimes they just killed them."

"How?"

"Well, sometimes, many times, they took them in a car to a secluded place, away from the city, along the road, and shot them."

"You were there?"

"No, they did not take me with them, but they told me later how they had done it. They seemed to need to tell me—I do not know why—how they had shot them in the head or through the heart. Maybe they just wanted to see my reaction, to make sure I was scared. I think they wanted me to fear them."

"Did you?"

"I did fear them, yes. But not too much, I think. Once they told me they had just returned from beating a woman to death."

"Good Lord."

"But then I began to see them as children. But of course, they were not children, they were just human. Like your agencies here, you know, the FBI and CIA, human and capable of anything. Yes, I did fear them. I was working for them. I mean, their business was not mine. I just worked for them. I was like a servant, you know?"

"Not a helper?" she asked. "You never helped them?" Then she waited for his defense. But it did not come. Oddly, he seemed to slump in his chair as he looked down at his cup.

"Yes," he replied softly. "Yes, I suppose I did."

She searched his face. "I mean, you said you photographed people they would then kill. That sounds like more than a servant, to me. That sounds like you were one of them. I mean, I'm sorry, you can use other words, but it seems like you were just one of them."

"Yes."

The reply was too simple. It was stupid, she thought, not at all what she wanted. The answer was wrong and the pain in his face was wrong. She was silent.

"Anyway," he said, "so much has changed. I suppose, it has changed, yes."

She blinked. "What has changed?"

"I mean, the world has changed. You know, since the Cold War is over, and everything, at least, I think it is over. Everyone says it is over. There was Gorby, all that, the failed coup, then I sort of woke up one day and Russia was just Russia."

"And?"

"Yes," he sighed. "Well, they still wanted me to work for them. They sent me everywhere, at least in Europe, lots of countries, cities mainly. Most of the projects were stupid, meaningless."

Here he chuckled cynically, and she thought she could despise him for it. She lifted her cup and sipped the coffee, convinced she could easily despise him.

He continued, "I would never have been good as a spy, anyway. I would have been like a bad actor, like a clown, very stupid. So, well, finally they started the Program, and since I knew a lot of languages and could mimic accents pretty well— maybe you do not think so—ha.—they moved me into the training." He shrugged. "Since I knew about Europe and the customs of a lot of countries, I guess it only made logical sense."

"Program?" she queried, leaning forward again. "What program was that?"

There it was, the placement of the critical query. All the skill she had exercised, all the effort she had made, all the patience she had shown, had led to this. She had acted her part, she had said her lines, now all she had to do was to listen. Relaxed, happy, she would just sip her coffee . . . and listen.

He pressed his hands together gently as if to pray. "The idea of the Program," he replied, "was, very simply, to send very huge number of Russian people to live in United States. It was intended for them to infiltrate the American society and yet remain always loyal to Russia, whether to old Russia or new Russia, did not matter, simply to Russia. They were to mix—*seamlessly*, is the word, yes—with every part of American culture, but remain always on the side of Russia for any vote and in any international dispute. The idea was that if Russian population could be increased here to many people, their influence, in voting, making money, or whatever, would be significant. This influence would then come down on the side of Russia, if crisis comes up, any kind of crisis, here in America or on international stage. And even if the crisis never comes up, that influence of Russian perspective in American life would benefit Russia."

She put her cup down. "You're talking about Communism?"

"But, yes, Communism is not as important as it used to be. Whichever way Russia goes in the future, she will always remain Russia. You know, even before Communism, the Russia of history— Russia."

"And you are definitely one of these people?"

He nodded. "Yes."

"And you're not a spy?"

"No."

"You're not here for any secrets?"

He shook his head. "No, no secrets, just to be the influence. We would become citizens, vote, enter the education, the arts, the police, the military, the politics, all levels of society. We would generate funds and send them back to our families, friends, whoever. But the funds were not to be the major thing. The major thing was influence of Russian mentality on America."

"So, you do this." She wrinkled her nose. "And you like doing this?"

He shrugged, not from indifference but from anxiety.

She shook her head, as if to clear it. "Good Lord. I don't really know what to say. You certainly know how to blow a person's mind on New Year's Eve."

He smiled. "That is a drug term, you know. It is from drug culture."

"I know."

"Everybody uses it, but it comes from drug culture, from LSD."

She did not reply.

He pushed his water glass with his forefinger. "I never took drugs."

Shaking her head, "Neither did I."

"But alcohol, yes?"

"Yes, of course, but within limits."

"Yes," he laughed. "Good."

"Why is that funny?" she asked.

Looking at her hair, "I do not know."

"I think you do," she insisted. "*Why?*"

He shrugged. "It is funny because I cannot imagine that you could do anything beyond the limits."

"Is that so?"

"Yes," he laughed. "You seem to have very controlled personality."

"It's voluntary, I assure you," she returned, lifting her cup again. "But I'm really curious, aren't you afraid that people will find out about you and tell the government—the FBI or the CIA?"

He gestured to indicate a negative. "No. They would not be able to do anything. I mean, your government."

"But they could deport you, isn't that right? They'd probably deport everyone they found."

"How? No, they are all here legally, and everything they do is legal. It would be illegal to deport them."

"That's a little naive, I think."

"Oh, yes," he continued. "I know, I know, yes. They would deport them, anyway. The word *legal* is a joke in America just like in Russia. But what I mean is, having so many of us here, all living within the law, is like having a lock on the door, it slows the thief down, you know?"

"But aren't the Russians afraid, um, your government, aren't they concerned that you might be won over to just being American?"

"And that means what? Walmart? No, these days you can get anything in Russia that you can get here."

"Except America," she replied.

"That is true, yes, you cannot get America in Moscow. But you can get anything else. Sometimes it costs more, but you can get it."

"America is more than prosperity."

"Yes, as you say, it is a way of life. And many people in the program will be attracted to that way of life, they will find it irresistible. I confess, *I* am attracted to it."

Then he grew quiet and she thought he looked small and sad, and she wondered what he was really after as a man and about his family and about all the things that might never be known about him, things that might show him to be someone different from the man she had been led to believe he was. Oh, they had been right about his being in the program. But what about the rest? What about the core human being that lived in the body?

"But," he continued, "it does not matter."

She sniffed. "I think it does," she retorted. "Actually, I think everything matters."

He looked again at her hair, which glowed, he thought, like the hair of an angel. "You may think it matters," he said, "but you cannot prove that it matters." When she did not respond he asked, "What would you offer as proof?"

Her coffee gone, she put the cup down and looked at him for a moment. "I would offer as proof the fact that there must be something—in all the world, there must be *something*—that matters. And if something matters, just one thing, anything at all, then everything does. What do you say to that?"

His eyes twinkled. "I would say, that you are more of an idealist than I am. You should have been a Communist."

Wincing, she did not respond.

"You know, many Russians love Russia and would not want to live anywhere else in the world, and yet also many Russians really just want to be Americans and live in America. They think like Americans. But, and I have found this to be true, there are also some Americans who would do extremely well to be living in Russia. Yes, that is correct—Mother Russia. I have met them. Some of them have never even been to Russia, and some of them, well, they are more Russian than I am."

"I doubt that," she returned sarcastically.

"Why?"

She shrugged, answering seriously, "You seem to be very Russian."

"Sometimes I am uncertain *what* I am."

"But uh, so, let me ask you something, aren't you a little afraid, I mean, telling me these things? You must have been sworn to secrecy."

"Yes," he nodded, "I am afraid."

"Your revealing it must be illegal."

Another nod. "Yes."

"Would they hurt you, their agents?"

"Only if they did not use a gun," he laughed. Then seriously he replied, "Possibly they would do it, probably they would not. It would not be worth it to them, I think. They have done the calculations and know what they want out of their effort. They will get it. The program will be successful, I think."

"So, you're not talking ideology, you're talking nationalism."

"Yes, exactly. Being Communist or Capitalist does not matter so much to them right now, but being Russian *does*."

Shaking her head, "Well, I hate to break it to you, but even here, pure nationalism can be a hard sell."

"I understand, but I think that some people, perhaps not very many, but enough to make difference, will always see the mystical qualities of their homeland, their motherland, their roots, as you say here. And I think that, especially in the crisis times, economic or whatever, everyone has tendency to cling to the earth, to defend the family, the house, the neighborhood, the city, the nation. So, there is always the basic people in society, who have the heart forever with the homeland. In times of crisis that sense of defense of the homeland spreads to everyone. But I think the theory behind this program I have told you about is that if Russia can infiltrate American society with people whose minds are deeply and truly Russian, well, you see, their influence, in whatever form, would be for Russia."

They fell silent as the server arrived with fresh coffee. There was no new singing from the bar area, and the people at the surrounding tables produced only a hum as they ate and chatted.

"Look," she said when the server had gone, "I don't know why you have told me all this. Just why *did* you tell me?"

For a moment he could only stare at her. Now not only her hair but all of her seemed to glow. In a subdued voice he replied, "I have found many wonderful things here in America, but now I have found something else."

"What is that?"

"You."

A moment passed before she was aware of her own surprise. She had been in control of everything. She had designed, executed, and nurtured their relationship in the usual way. She had heard and processed all the information in the usual way. In fact, everything had been done according to plan and nothing had been left beyond the circle of predictability. No one should have been surprised by anything. But now she was surprised, though not by his words, but by her own vulnerability.

"You found me," she repeated. "What does that mean?"

"It means," he replied, "that I have fallen in love with you."

She could not resist dropping her gaze. Without looking up, she said softly, "I'm sorry, Stanley, I don't know what to say. I just have no response." But she knew that she was lying and that from somewhere in the deepest part of her, beyond the authority of her intellect, a response had indeed been made. Then she lifted her eyes to his.

"You do not have to say anything," he said. "It is all right, you do not have to say anything at all."

But then she did say something, something very real. "You know my age. Are you sure you want to love a woman ten years older than you?"

Shaking his head slowly, "No, I am not sure, and I do not want to love you. But I do love you. Very simply, I do."

She could not look at him, so she looked past him, to where the server had gone to the kitchen. Life was so very odd, she thought, how it sang and danced before you until you were thoroughly confused. It offered you things you should desire and when you acquiesced and had eventually acquired them it took them away. It showed you things to be afraid of and when you acquiesced and had eventually acquired security against those things it gave them to you anyway. In all of it life seemed mischievously intent upon promulgating its malignancy in your existence. It wanted to use you and then ruin you. Worst of all, it demanded your heart, only to destroy your love heartlessly. No wonder people said you couldn't win. Now she looked back at him, into his candid face, his honest eyes. Carefully she lifted the napkin from her lap, folded it in half, and placed it beside the dessert plate.

"Can I ask you to do something?" she queried, with a simple smile of acquiescence.

"Yes," he answered. "Yes, you can ask me, yes."

"Would you come and kiss me?"

As if performing a rite, he pushed himself away from the table, stepped behind her chair, and helped as she pushed it back. As she turned he took her left hand in his right, slid his left hand around her waist to her back, and pressed all of her gently to himself as he kissed her.

CHAPTER 6

New Year's Day 2008

"You came home last night a little rosier in the cheeks than usual, dear," Maggie said as Martina's blue corduroy robe passed her chair. After no response, she repeated, with emphasis, "*Rosier.*"

The kitchen was warm, as Maggie liked it, but after taking a seat, Martina still adjusted the heavy material to expose less of her neck. Finally she replied disinterestedly, "Yes?"

Frowning, "Do you know you have ten robes? I only have one, and you have ten."

"You could have ten if you wanted, Maggie."

"But I only need one."

Martina put her elbows on the table, rested her chin upon the backs of her fingers, and in silence looked into the suspicious green eyes.

Maggie shrugged. "Definitely, rosier than usual."

"Why didn't you say something last night—you know, ask me if I'd been between the sheets with him?"

Ignoring the question, "And it wasn't terribly late."

Martina sighed. "Every place was full, and there wasn't anything to do after dinner."

"You could have gone to a movie."

"We considered it, but then just drove around in the city and came home."

"Really?"

Annoyed, Martina did not respond, peering again into the green eyes.

Adjusting her own robe, Maggie tucked one leg under and offered, "Sounds like, you're not the luckiest person in the world, then." It was a favorite expression. It meant nothing, as they both knew, but was merely something to say as part of the tapestry of the conversation. Somehow, even after countless uses of the expression, Maggie enjoyed hearing herself say it again. Then she said, "Well, not to change the subject, of course, because it's all very interesting and tantalizing, and your use of the term *between the sheets* just gives me a thrill, but let me ask you, if you don't mind my being professional, how about the information, did you make any progress there? Are you all right, dear? You seem blanched."

Avoiding the latter question, Martina answered, "Maybe I made a little progress. Is there anything to eat? And when is the meeting, did you get everyone?"

"Yes, Friday. Everybody's good for then. Friday evening, here."

"This is Tuesday. Yes, that's fine."

Maggie frowned. "Actually, I thought you'd be upset, want it moved up to tomorrow night or something."

"I can wait."

Maggie bristled with sarcasm. "That's right, you did take the time to go to Vermont."

No response.

Maggie smiled. "You're annoyed, dear."

"*I'm* annoyed? I think *you* are. What's wrong with being rosy?"

"Rosi*er*," Maggie corrected, "is what I said, I think."

"But what is *wrong* with being rosier?"

Ignoring the question, Maggie said, "Okay, Friday it is. I'll confirm it. Are you going out today?"

"No, I'm tired. I think I'll watch the parade or just relax, maybe read."

Sarcastically again, "Read? You'd be able to concentrate?"

"Why wouldn't I be able to concentrate?"

"I don't know, maybe because of mister Moscow."

"No," replied Martina in a benign tone, "I'll be okay. Are you going out?"

"I'll probably just stay here and watch you watch the parade."

"Anyway," Martina chuckled, "I'm still asking if there's anything to eat."

"There are pancakes warming in the oven, dear. Would you like pancakes?"

"Wonderful, yes. And then I suppose I'll put a little distance behind me on the treadmill."

"Is the basement a place for a pretty girl on New Year's Day?"

They did not usually watch the New Year's Day parade, and there was nothing to draw them to it this year, except perhaps the novelty of seeing it on the new set's glitzy screen. As the parade unfolded its storybook of floats, clowns, cowboys both women were mesmerized by the magnificent, glowing images.

"Your phone, dear," said Maggie.

Fumbling to read the caller's identity and avoid Maggie's inquisitive scrutiny at the same time, Martina finally opened the instrument and held it to her ear. "Hi, Stanley," she said, pulling a cushion close to snuggle. "Listen, why don't I call you back in a few minutes, would that be okay? . . . Sure. . . . Thanks."

"Is he going to want to see you today?" Maggie asked.

"I think so. Is that all right?"

An impatient sigh. "Why wouldn't it be?"

Hugging the cushion. "Sorry, Maggie."

"It would have been nice to laze around here. We could watch a movie."

"I can stay."

Annoyed, "No, you should go, to keep the momentum going."

Martina gave her head a shake. "Maggie, what is it? First you seem almost jealous when I go out with Mr. Osipov, then you seem anxious to get the information, and now you want me to stay home and watch movies. It's a little confusing."

"It's fine, it's okay, and I may just go out anyway, so you should go call him."

Waiting for him was like waiting for Father the night of the escape. But finally he came and she moved the curtain to watch him climb the steps.

They drove to his house in Olney, for she had asked to see where he lived and where he did his photography. Somehow she was not surprised to find that the entire house functioned as his studio. Boxes, materials, equipment, were everywhere. Tripods and studio lamps stood everywhere, and she took his hand as he led her around them to an old couch.

"Here, sit here," he said. "Would you like tea or coffee, something else?"

"Tea would be nice," she replied as she sat.

He continued to talk from the kitchen as he prepared the tea. She could tell from the way he opened and shut the cabinets, clinked the cups, moved about, that he was nervous. But it did not occur to her to exploit his anxiety, not anymore. Instead, she busied herself with fantasies of straightening up the living room, putting things in order, even cleaning. She had never been domestic in her thinking, but now the idea of cleaning his house seemed quite natural and attractive to her.

Then he walked in with a tray of tea, grinning like a child, proud that he had prepared it.

"How do you like my house?" he asked, setting the tray upon a cardboard box and beaming at her. "Is it what you expected? Tell me. You can tell me, I won't be offended."

"No, it's charming," she answered, sitting forward.

Leaving a place between them, he sat at the end of the couch. "You probably think it is very messy. And it is, I know. Here, take your cup." He poured the tea and passed it to her.

"This is your equipment?" she queried, looking at the menagerie of material that crowded the room.

"There is more," he answered, taking a cup for himself and then relaxing into the corner of the couch, "but I left it in Russia. I visit there and play with it, like toys. Here, would you like to have a cookie?" Pulling the package open, he held it out to her.

She took one and sat back.

"Why did you want to see my house?" he asked, chuckling. "Did you want to see if I was a pig?"

"I guess I did, yes, a little."

"Ha—I knew it. But that is all right. I am a pig sometimes. I am happy you came out with me today."

"Well, aren't you going to show me the rest of the house?"

"There is nothing else to see," he replied. "You can see it if you want to, but it is not interesting and it is all a little messy. I can show you everything, but there is nothing much to see. I sleep upstairs in a messy bed. I wash laundry things in the basement, also messy."

"I like it here. It's peaceful. Do you like the neighborhood?"

"Not so much, no."

"Sorry."

He shrugged and again grinned. "I will move sometime."

She looked at him for a moment and then said, "I like a living room with a carpet and warm chairs. I like furniture, carpets, curtains, things like that."

He nodded. "Yes, I know you like those things."

She sipped her tea, then said, "It's funny how we adjust as humans."

He smiled.

"Where will you go when you move?"

"I do not know," he replied with a shrug. "I will get a map."

"Yes."

"We are doing the small talk."

She nodded. "I would think you could call it that."

"Small talk is very historic. The whole world seems to have the small talk. Do you think small talk is good?"

"Well, if it isn't," she replied with a sigh, "it's at least necessary, don't you think?"

He did not answer, but then said, his voice soft, his eyes upon her teacup, "I remember last night as a beautiful dance."

"We didn't dance."

"No," he whispered, keeping his eyes on her cup.

Setting the cup upon the tray. "What else do you remember?"

Then he looked at her. "About last night?"

"Well, about life."

"Life. What does that mean?"

"*Your* life—I'd like to hear more about your life, your background." Then, when he seemed about to answer, she added, "You know, last night was wonderful. And what you said to me was wonderful."

"Yes, I agree, it was wonderful. I did mean what I said to you."

"I know."

"I am sorry," he said. "I should have told you more things, and I will tell you anything you want to know. But I did mean what I said to you."

"I know."

Then he got up and went to the front window and looked out toward the park across the street. When he first moved into the house he did this out of curiosity, but soon he did it as a kind of therapy for stress. He watched now as two women walked together, each with a dog on a leash.

"What is it?" she asked.

"Just people walking their dogs," he answered, still watching. "It makes me happy to see parks in the city. It is not just a place to walk dogs, it is a place where animals can get away, escape, and hide. About one month ago I saw two people stop their car across the street there and let a cat out onto the ground. Then they drove away. When the car was gone the cat ran off into the trees and then up the hill. It was December, very cold, and it was just a little cat."

He was a curious man, she thought, as she watched him put his hands on his head. He seemed unique in nearly everything about him, the way he carried himself, expressed himself, what he was willing to say and do.

"I'm sorry," she replied sympathetically. "People can be cruel."

He turned just briefly to look at her, and then he looked out through the glass again. "You know, I did not do anything."

"About the cat?"

"Yes. I did nothing."

She reached to pour more tea into her cup. "What could you have done?" she asked, raising the lid of the little pot. Inside, four tea bags lay in the dark brew. Replacing the lid, she simply sat back. "You said it ran away. What was there to do?"

"I could have gone out to look for him. I could have gotten my coat on and just gone out and called to him, or something. I could have taken some food out. I don't know. I could have done something. But I didn't do anything."

"Yes?"

"I abandoned him, too. They did and I did."

"That's stretching it, I think. I'm sorry, but I can't see that."

"Maybe I was supposed to see it happen, so I would help him, to bring him in out of the cold, you know. And I just did not do a thing. I think he froze to death."

She sighed heavily. "If I saw things that way, I'd feel guilty every day, just because I didn't stop to help some cat or dog. I've seen countless strays around the city. I don't stop or take them home with me. If I did, I'd have a house full of dogs and cats. You're not even allowed to do that. That's what taxes are for. The city takes care of it."

He nodded but did not look at her.

"You're blaming yourself," she continued, "for something that really wasn't your business."

"I suppose that you are correct," he admitted. "It was God's business, I guess."

"No. Well, I mean, sort of, yes, but things like that are the city's business. That's what we pay taxes for, it's part of the system, and that's what the system's for, to help on a large scale. The shelters are full of cats and dogs. The city does a good job."

He turned from the window, an unhappy smile on his face. "And you trust the system to help the individual?"

She wanted to respond, but could only return his smile. Then she said, "But you're blaming yourself, not the system."

"Yes," he admitted. "Yes, I am blaming me."

"Did you think like this when you were young, as a child?"

He shrugged, as if it was a response for himself alone. "I remember my mother," he said, "when I blundered in on her bath time, the beautiful white skin of her back, her startled eyes when she turned to look at me. I remember she was not sure what to think of the drawings I made of it later. She did not care, she said, but I could tell she was cautious. I remember my father, so strong and courageous. He would come home from the great Red Army, that is exactly what we called it, and he would talk endlessly about politics, spitting his hatred of Capitalism and greedy people. I listened and listened. Still, anyway, I admired him. And I remember my brothers, one older brother and one younger brother. They wanted to go to school and achieve. They never said what they wanted to achieve. I remember being the middle son—that meant something I never understood. But I remember that I had not a single vision whatever of life. I had not one idea what I wanted to do for an occupation in life. I was content to look at my mother's beautiful skin, listen to my father boast of his exploits and expound his political views, and admire my brothers as they prepared for school and the military. I was content with all of it, simply as it was. So, you ask if I was like this as a child. I do not know it. I did not even know I *was* a child, for most of the time. Does this make sense to you?"

She looked at him for a moment, a blank expression on her face. "Well, I can see you were probably the odd man out."

"What is this *odd man out*?" he said with a laugh. "Yes, I think I have heard it."

Her face still blank, "It means, you were seen as the strange one in your family, the one that didn't fit in."

He nodded. "Yes, this is what I was. It is a good expression, I will try to remember it."

Then she asked, "You lived in Moscow?"

"Yes, I liked it, it is perfect there, *idyllic* is the English word. I know it is filthy and clogged with traffic, but I love Russia, so I love Moscow. Russians know, you are nothing unless you live in Moscow. I do not believe that, of course, but I like it there. I go back one time every year to see my mother." And then, looking at her hair, he asked, "What do *you* remember? Tell me. I mean, please, I would like to know it. I would like to know more.

I do not need to know more, but I would like to. So, please."

"I remember last night," she replied.

He looked at her for a long time, then asked, "Can I show you something?"

From a group of thick and worn portfolios that lay on the wide work table he withdrew a bright-red one and flipped open its cover. She stood beside him and watched his hands, his facial expressions, as he held each photograph for her to see.

"These pictures were taken on a farm near St. Petersburg. It is not really a farm, it is more like a tract of land. Russia does not have farms like you have here, but you would call it a farm. Russia has the immense land. Friends of my parents own this farm. They are quite elderly. They invite me to visit whenever I can. I took these pictures there about ten years ago. They had twelve dogs, do you believe it, yes? Incredible. I love dogs. Look at them, they are magnificent, yes?"

She poked him with her finger. "Well, I guess I have to say yes, don't I?"

"No, really," he laughed, pulling away. "Just look. Really, they are wonderful."

She laughed with him then, freely, as if she had been laughing all day. She watched his lip curl, and the moment they were living through together seemed beautiful. And then he seemed beautiful, too, and the farm seemed beautiful, and certainly the dogs, with which he had clearly fallen in love, they seemed beautiful, too.

"Yes," she agreed, laughing helplessly, "they are wonderful dogs, gorgeous." And they laughed together again. "And did they chase that bear?" she asked, pointing to a framed photograph behind him, in which a bear lay in the snow. "You're a hunter?"

He did not look at the picture on the wall but away from it, away from everything, even away from her. Life was like that, it often made you have to look away from it. But then he looked, fixing his eyes upon it, and replied, "No, I am not a hunter. That was a bear I met in Siberia. I was on assignment with agents who were looking for a criminal. Ha—I have wondered how you get to be placed in those categories. I suppose, if you agree enough with a large enough entity, you are made an agent, and if you disagree enough you are made a criminal. Life is very bipolar, yes?"

She could only agree. For most of her life, even until just a few weeks ago, before she had been assigned to this Russian man, this target of hers, she would have disagreed. She would have said that people were sometimes bipolar, but life, never so. But life was like that then, it was only intentional, never magical.

"Anyway, so," he continued, forcing himself to speak, "we left the car and walked into the forest, not far. We were looking for the house and had to walk the distance—um, a distance. The fresh snow was everywhere, but we could walk on it. Suddenly, we came around a boulder and saw this bear, right in front of us. He was not very large, but he was a bear, you know. I do not know what he was doing, maybe looking for food. He did not seem to be hostile or angry, just surprised. We were, too. He stood up a little, half up, and looked at us. Then, and all of this happened in just moments, then one of the agents drew his pistol, an old Tokarev, and shot the bear in the face. The bear was startled, absolutely shocked. The agent laughed and then fired again into the bear's face. The bear seemed completely confused. He looked at me, not the man who shot him, but at *me*, as if to ask why he was being hurt. He was stunned and shook his head rapidly, fast, really fast. The man laughed again and then fired all the gun into the bear's head. Some of the bullets missed, I am sure, but the Tokarev is a very powerful weapon. The bear swayed a little, like he was drunk, still half standing up, and kept shaking his head. Then he just dropped, down into the snow. I took the photograph, and other photographs, not many. The agents decided to go back to the car, since there might be other bears close to us. They never found the criminal. They told me they were not very interested in catching him. Sometime after that, I went back to Moscow."

She wanted to speak, and then to touch him, but could only watch him as he stood staring down at the floor. It was a pathetic story, but this man seemed even more pathetic than the story, and the pathos of his sadness seemed to grip her fiercely, as if to mandate her silence.

Then he raised his head and continued. "I remember lying in the bed that night, after coming back from the bear. I asked myself why I was any better than that bear, why my fate should be any better than that bear's fate. And I kept picturing how the bear looked at me, as though I was somehow responsible. I could not sleep. All night I just stayed there awake in the bed, thinking about him lying in the snow, his eyes closed, snowflakes on his snout, blood all around his head. I kept thinking of him lying out in the forest, frozen in the snow beside the boulder, with nothing around him but the cold trees and the endless snow. Every snowflake in the world is special. Every snowflake in that forest and on the fur of the bear's face was special. Each snowflake has a unique pattern and is so beautiful that it changes your heart as you look at it. I thought about him all night. I thought about how he was out in the snow, but I was in the warm bed. I kept seeing his face as he was being shot and the way he looked at me. You ask what I remember? That is what I remember."

"But," she reasoned, sighing heavily, "you didn't shoot him, you just took his picture. You didn't have a gun, you had a camera."

He was silent.

"You didn't even *decide* to shoot him," she continued. "You *wouldn't* have shot him."

"I am not exactly certain that matters."

Now she was able to reach out, and she put her hand upon his arm. "No," she said. "No, I can see it doesn't matter. With the cat, it was responsibility, but with the bear, just the tragedy of it."

He shrugged. "I do not really know. I am as confused as the bear was, I think."

"But you blame yourself, anyone can see that. And you're not going to forgive yourself, are you?"

Then she returned to the couch, watching him as he replaced the photos and the portfolio. He was pathetic, slouching there in his pain, but there was nowhere else she wanted to look. She could not tell herself she had simply grown fond of him. Suddenly she felt helpless, as when reaching out futilely to help someone in a dream. It was difficult for her even to move, but she got up and went to him and stood beside him and then turned him to face her.

"People can change," she said. "They can overcome guilt, they can forgive other people, and they can forgive themselves. They can forgive, or they can become victims." And when he leaned close and touched her nose with his lips so softly that she could not close her eyes, she said, without thinking, "You know, at five nine you're just over my height. In these half-heels I am exactly your height. Our lips meet when we're standing."

"I can see that they do, yes," he returned. But then he asked, "How did you know I was five feet nine inches tall?"

Slowly she exhaled, as if the air that left her lungs had a terrible weight to it. "Actually, Stanley, I have been hoping that you would come to ask something like that."

He shook his head. "What do you mean?"

Returning to the couch, she sat and then with her hand touched lightly the place beside her. "Please, please come and sit," she said softly. She watched as he walked slowly toward her and sat, his face suddenly bloodless.

He stared and his voice was ominous, "Why do you want me to sit here?"

She waited for just a moment and then answered, "Because I want to do something illegal."

"I would like to have my answer, Martina," he said firmly. "How did you know my height? You said it like you knew it precisely. So? How?"

She had not thought that she would be relaxed, but she was. Her eyes moved over him as gently as his lips had touched her nose. Then she said, "Our first meeting in the video store was not by chance." And when she saw his eyes begin to work from side to side, she added, "It was intentional."

"Which, could mean many things," he said cautiously.

"Stanley, it was planned."

With his eyes locked upon her, he asked, "What are you saying to me?"

"I'm saying, it was planned by others, a team."

"Please say more."

"Is anyone else here, in the house?"

"No one," he answered, his face blank.

"I am an advisor to the CIA."

As if through the lips of a corpse, he replied, "True?"

She nodded. "Yes, it's true, it's very true."

Incredulous, he sighed, as if in defeat. "Please, tell me, please."

"I will, even now as we sit here on your couch, in your house, in your world. You confessed to me last night, and I am confessing to you now. I am an advisor to the CIA, assigned to Mr. Stanley Osipov." And there she left it, positioned tenderly on the equation pad of his mind. The report had stated that he was oddly simple, yet very intelligent, at once capable of holding naive beliefs and of making correct calculations at electric speed. She believed he would not disappoint her. He did not.

"Obviously you are saying, Martina, that you love me."

Eyes closed, she whispered, "Yes."

He nodded and looked away. "Your admission—"

"Confession," she corrected, searching the blue eyes.

"Your confession has made you a criminal, since you must have been sworn to secrecy."

She gave the slightest affirmative nod.

"And there is only one thing that could have made you tell me this."

"Yes," she whispered again.

"Love."

She nodded, with a smile. "My program monitors your program. From the CIA's perspective, I have compromised the entire program. They will never believe that I have not told you everything I know about CIA operations."

"You have not told me about the way things work, and please do not tell me. They will think you have told me more, but do not do it."

"In their eyes," she said, "for me to tell you anything is to tell you everything, and to tell you, is to tell your people. That's the way they have to think, it's the way we think as part of them. We can't blame them. I would see it the same way. I know that my telling you what I did, was illegal, I know that, I said it was."

"Do not worry," he replied, "my people will see me the same way, and they will not be happy. They will think that I have told you everything."

CHAPTER 7

For Martina and Maggie the remainder of New Year's week was viciously frustrating. It seemed to be a principle that the Christmas break worked like an eraser on the middle-school student mind, wiping it, like a blackboard, nearly clean, leaving only traces of what it had learned from September to the Christmas break. For Martina and Maggie the only strategy that had ever worked for mending this effect of the holidays was immediate and concentrated reiteration of material. Of course, this required evenings of rigorous preparation.

For Stanley the week's schedule was equally demanding. He had accepted an offer from one of the city's leading newspapers to fill in for a staff photographer too hungover from the holidays to work. Usually he enjoyed such assignments, since 'temping' often allowed him to get at the real soul of city life. But now his concentration seemed to be off in everything he did. Throughout an entire day's shooting he had worked with the camera set wrong, so that in the evening nearly every shot showed digital blur on the computer. Yes, his concentration was definitely off. In fact, since Martina's confession on New Year's Day he had been able to think of little else but her and the events of that afternoon.

On Friday evening Martina's team assembled as planned. Maggie let the other members in at just after seven and took their coats. The four sat in their usual places around the coffee table in the front room, munching cookies and chatting. The previous three days had been a frenetic return to school for all of them.

"Why," asked Maggie, arriving from the kitchen with a laden tray, "are teachers forced to resort to punishing an entire class when only one student is guilty, just because we can't find out who the guilty person is?"

After positioning the tray at the center of the table, she superfluously adjusted its four bowls of fruit, nuts, crackers, and pastry, then gave the cozied coffee and tea pots a fine tune to make everything more presentable. Satisfied, she smoothed the sleeves of her cashmere sweater and took her usual place on the couch.

Gretchin, at the other end of the couch, watched her as she sat. Pushing a handful hair behind an ear, she responded, "Who's forcing you? Just let it go."

"Yes, you could do that," returned Maggie, reaching for a saucer and cup. For some reason, perhaps as a reward for carrying the tray, she would not stand upon ceremony and wait for her guests, but would pour herself a cup of tea. "But then the student could easily circumvent the power of the system."

"Oh, come on."

Maggie's cup clinked upon the saucer. "No, a bad student can simply hide within the group, knowing the teacher never can keep an eye on everyone."

Gretchin shrugged. "Who cares? Just let it go. Catch the ones you can and let the others get away with whatever. Do what you can and walk away from it. You can't catch everyone."

Bradley, who hated the sound of clinking china, frowned and then pointed with his finger. "You can catch more than you'd think, people, let me tell you. Never give up. You can get them."

"It's unfair," Martina put in, reaching for a cup and saucer. "Punishing a class of thirty because you don't know who the one culprit is, means that ninety-seven percent of the class is punished when they're innocent. They didn't do anything."

"Exactly," agreed Gretchin, following, with a perfunctory smile, the sheen of Martina's platinum hair. She wondered if her own hair would look as good when she reached Martina's age.

"But if you don't do it," said Maggie, "if you don't somehow weed out the culprit, the other bad students get bolder. And bad behavior usually doesn't level off, it escalates. Now, tell me that doesn't take at least some control away from the teacher and place it in the hands of a few bad kids. It actually harms the other students. All educators know this."

"Fine," said Martina, "so, that teaches the students what about the system? That it has to incorrectly punish twenty-nine innocent people in order to correctly punish one guilty person."

Bradley frowned. "Well, it's not easy being a policeman, and that's what we are, face it. Every educator is a cop, that's just the way it is. Nobody really *wants* to do the job. But kids have to be taught. And you have to keep order or you can't teach them, right? I mean, that's right."

Martina looked at Maggie and rolled her eyes. "But that's what I'm saying, Bradley," she replied. "*What* are they being taught? That the justice system they're expected to believe in has an error rate of ninety-seven percent? And that that error rate is actually *required* for success in achieving justice? Anybody with even average intelligence will eventually see that that's a pretty inefficient system."

He shrugged. "You have no choice."

Then Maggie said, "That was my point. The teacher feels *forced*."

"Yes," he chimed confidently. "And it can't be helped. If a teacher has to give detention to the whole class in order to catch the unknown culprit, it has to be done, that's all. We're expected to control our classrooms." Here his tone became somewhat pastoral. "And I think the good students would rather have the teacher control the class than have the class manipulated by a few bad students. It can't be helped. If you have to give detention or whatever to the whole class when you don't know who the culprit is, just do it. Absolutely. Don't even think about it." And with this he placed the remnants of a cookie into his mouth and began to chew with relish, to indicate he considered the matter settled.

"I know the logic of that position," complained Maggie, "but I also know that I hate being blamed for something someone else has done. I just hate it."

Swallowing awkwardly, he licked a crumb from his lip. "I know, Maggie. It's like shotgunning a crowd to stop a fleeing thief. It's terribly unfair. But you know, the crowd is not all that innocent, either. I mean, each one of them has stolen something, too. They just were never caught when they deserved it."

As Martina placed a small cushion at the middle of her back, her eyes again met Maggie's and this time communicated incredulity. Neither of them had ever cared for this man. With disdain they had observed his assumption of the leadership of their quiet middle school. Both she and Maggie considered him a pathetic mechanist. They saw him as a man with a head as big as a football and filled with as much substance.

Gretchin, savoring the bouquet of her tea, reiterated, "I say, just let them go. It's not important."

"No," he insisted. "You've got to catch them. You've got to get them. It *is* important."

"No, it isn't," she said. "Who gives a shit in hell, anyway?"

He straightened his back. "You know, Gretchin, I hope you don't talk like that around the students."

"Well, you'll just have to put your goddamn ear to the keyhole, won't you?"

"You're not being funny, Gretchin."

Deliberately Martina lifted the teapot from the tray. "More tea?" she asked. "Help yourselves to everything, please, there's a lot here. Thanks for bringing it, everyone, as usual." Then she set the pot down, straightened its cozy, and said, "Okay. I suppose we should get started. As you know, my preliminary findings suggested that Mr. Osipov was a genuine infiltration immigrant. Thanks for changing plans so you could meet him at the party after my first contact. That was really helpful in speeding things up. Anyway, I told Richard I thought the Agency's suspicions were justified and that Mr. Osipov was the real thing."

Producing a sly smile, Bradley interjected, "And of course he backed you."

The movement in her eyes was imperceptible. She replied, "Yes, Bradley, he did."

"And why not?" he continued. "Your score is perfect. You're batting a thousand."

Maggie quipped meekly, "We don't watch baseball."

"So," Martina continued, "Richard said to go ahead and make plans to snag Mr. Osipov."

Gretchin chuckled. "It's the usual, then? He's not trading secrets?"

Martina smiled. "No secrets. He's just here to work and vote and become one of us."

Gretchin pushed the hair back again. "Is he bad?"

"Meaning?"

"Is he bad? Is he a bad man? You know what I mean. Does he have bad character?"

Bradley, his elbow resting comfortably upon the armrest of his chair, broke in, "Gretch, he wouldn't be here if he had good character, think about it."

Martina felt certain no one had seen her wince at this, but was incorrect. When she looked up she saw Maggie's inquisitive eyes peering at her.

Gretchin tucked a leg under. "But is he bad?"

Martina said softly, "No, Gretchin, he's not."

"So, he's not going to hurt anybody."

"I don't think so."

"Is he armed?"

Martina sighed and then shook her head. "I don't know. I honestly don't. Richard said he wasn't."

"But they've been wrong."

"What's your point?"

The shoulders lifted beneath the ringlets, which had fallen from behind the ear again. "Well, if he's not going to hurt anybody, why not speed things up?"

"Meaning?"

The shoulders lifted again briefly. "You know, give him a call."

From his chair across from her Bradley scrunched his brow. "And ask him what?"

The aqua eyes rolled with unbelief. "If he wants a piece of ass, stupid. And then get him to talk."

Looking away quickly, he said, "Gretchin, that's disgusting."

"Is it?" she shot back. "It works, *Brad.*"

Her disdain for him was so obvious that he could muster only a glance in her direction. He swore to himself that never in God's world would he put up with such disrespect in the school setting, but then reminded himself that as a CIA advisory team they were an autonomous entity, presently led by Martina and ultimately controlled by Richard.

Straightening his shirt front, he asked, as if the exchange with Gretchin had not taken place, "What I don't understand is why they don't just tap or record these people more? I mean, when they're sure, like we are."

Martina recalled her own frustration at the restaurant. She shrugged and merely said, "I've wondered the same myself. There must be problems with the legality of it, and also with funding, probably."

"But they don't let us record them at all. I mean, *we've* never done it, right?"

"Well," said Gretchin, "we would know that, wouldn't we, Brad?"

He frowned. "You don't need to be smart, I think. The point is, they don't let us record them. And we could prove the whole thing with that."

"Why would we need to?" asked Maggie. "We've got Martina." And then she added, "And she's batting a thousand, remember?"

He sighed with irritation, but did not respond.

Martina scratched her knee elegantly. "I know it's frustrating. But there's no immediate threat or dealing in secrets. And the Russian program's huge, they're all over the place. So, I think the Agency just wants to pick out a few, deport them, send a message. I don't think they prove anything, just threaten them and send them home. The Russians know the only thing illegal about the program is the conspiracy part. And who's going to prove that or fund getting rid of it? Right now, the Agency just wants to slow them down. And that's where we come in, as you know. The Agency must have hundreds of teams like ours."

He had been watching her lips as she spoke. Then he looked at his shoe. "Why did Richard pick us, do you think, I mean, initially? Why did he approach us, of all people, three public school teachers and a principal?"

"Who knows?" she returned, annoyed. "But it is a perfect cover, you have to admit."

"I agree," said Gretchin, "although we are a little dysfunctional. Well," giving Bradley a look, "among ourselves."

"Yes," he retorted, "but everybody irritates *you*, face it."

"You might be right," she returned, giving the hair another push. "God, you people are slow sometimes."

Ignoring this, Martina continued, "Well, I do know why Richard wanted *me* to make the contact with Mr. Osipov. It was because of my age. Richard told me Mr. Osipov had shown a fondness for his mother and was believed to be attracted to older women."

Gretchin raised her eyebrows. "And *is* he?"

"Perhaps," she answered coolly.

Sitting forward, Maggie lowered her eyelids halfway, so that the green of her eyes seemed to glow through the ominous slits. "Tell them, dear, my theory as to why Richard recruited the four of us to be a team."

Martina hesitated. "No, you go ahead."

Then, leaning forward, as if about to stand, Maggie said, "Actually, I think it was because we all had a *reason*."

In the silent aftermath Gretchin spoke. "A reason? Explain, please."

"A reason to hate the Communists."

"What do you mean? Everybody hates them, it's part of the culture, like wearing a baseball cap. What do you mean, a reason?"

"Well, not just a common reason. A particular reason." She smiled briefly and continued. "Each of us has a particular reason for hating the Communists." Then she sat back, crossed her legs, and began to smooth the plush gray corduroy of her pants.

Gretchin returned impatiently, "Mysteries are fun, Maggs, but I don't want to try to solve one right now. Why don't you *explain,* this time?"

Quelling her pleasure at this, for she loved setting people up, Maggie lifted her chin and said, "The Agency has our complete histories. And not just on file. They are experts at histories. They know all about the escape of Martina's family from East Germany, that her mother had died there because the Communists would not provide the medicine she needed. They know that Martina's father then defected, with his children, not in hope but as a broken man." For a moment she looked at Martina, and then continued. "My own father worked for British Intelligence on the continent in the Cold War. Needless to say, I rarely saw him." For some reason she seemed to need to stop and smile. "Then a friend of our family, one of my father's colleagues, was *lost* at a checkpoint. He was shot. And there is Gretchin, born in Stockholm. Her uncle on her mother's side was married to a Finn and became a snow sniper when the Soviets invaded. But he was captured by the Russians and executed on the spot." Here she glanced at Bradley, who sat looking at his shoe. "And Bradley's father," she said simply, "was shot through the heart by a North Vietnamese Regular." As she finished her hand was still smoothing the corduroy. Her skin shining eerily in the soft light, she concluded with, "That, really, is my case."

For a moment, only the silence was audible.

Bradley pulled at a shoe string. Imagining his father in battle, he said, "It sounds plausible. I guess, it really sounds plausible. But how did we end up in the same workplace, a small suburban school?"

"Coincidence," Maggie offered, shrugging. "Richard just got lucky, probably. But when he read the histories of those he was recruiting, he knew we were perfect for going after the Russians."

"But I never knew my uncle," said Gretchin. "I was born much later. My father told us about him, but I don't have an emotional connection with his memory, or anything."

"But he was family," said Maggie. "In your case and mine the relationship may be more remote, but in Richard's mind we all had a particular reason to hate the Communists. That's why he wanted us to work together, like wolves."

"Maggie," said Martina patiently, "I know this theory means a lot to you, and maybe it's correct, but what difference does it make? We still have to deal with the assignments, and the latest is Mr. Osipov. Even if we were picked as wolves, we still have to complete the assignment."

Maggie's ascent was halfhearted. "True, dear," she replied simply and sipped her tea.

"Incidentally," Martina said to everyone, "not all these people are Communists, we know that. Most of them are a mixed bag. Russia's a mix."

"You mean, mixed up," Bradley quipped.

"Yes, well, who isn't?" she returned.

He straightened his jaw. "Personally, I view Russia and Communism as synonymous."

"History doesn't agree."

"Oh, come on, Martina, their transition to Communism was a walk in the park."

"Again, history does not agree."

His tone became challenging. "I don't care what history says. For the Russians to accept Communism at all, means that's what they always were and always will be. I see the two as married. And not only married, but meant for each other. And I don't care what the current Russian trend is. They can play with Capitalism, but it's just theater."

She smiled. "But that's a viewpoint, just a viewpoint. Another viewpoint is that the Russians were just playing with Communism, that it was an experiment, and that the Russian people have really been Capitalists all along. And besides, for most people, the distinctions between the ideologies are not as important as they used to be."

"No, no, no," he retorted, "they'll always be important. The stuff never goes away. It's like a virus that's always in the bloodstream of some people. You can fight Communism, you can laugh at Communism, but it'll always be there, and it'll come out. It looks for a weak economy, and there it is."

Then Gretchin said, "Let me ask you something, Bradley. What would you say the real difference is between Americans and Russians?"

His eyes went to the ceiling. "Gretchin, you are so lame."

"Look," she shot back, "don't talk to me that way, fucker, get it? You talk down to me all the time. Jesus, I hate that, so fucking stop it, okay?"

He was silent for a moment, then said, "You don't have to talk like that."

"Yeah? And you don't have to piss me off either. I was asking you a philosophical question, so just give me your answer, okay?"

"Well," he replied, "I think the difference between Americans and Russians is that we're the good guys and they're the bad guys, it's as simple as that."

"So, you're saying they're dangerous?"

"Yes, they're dangerous, of course they are."

"And Mr. Osipov?"

"Of course."

Martina smoothed a wrinkle in her sweater. "It doesn't matter. We're not really spies, we're observers, advisors, as Maggie continually reminds me."

Chuckling with unbelief, he said, "I love that. You're not a spy, Martina? You? Come on, what a deception."

"No," she answered coolly, "I am not. I don't have the coldness for it, for one thing."

He leveled his eyes at her. "You're like ice, Martina, *dry* ice."

She was unperturbed. "Bradley, I wouldn't make things more sinister than they are. We have a simple assignment with Mr. Osipov, as we did with the others—get the information the Agency needs to put him out of the country. So, let's keep things in that context."

He made no reply to this, but he wondered how many times she had sniggled like a rat on such simple assignments in order to get the information for the Agency. He wondered how many lies she had told and men she had slept with just to get that information. He did not believe there were many women who could sleep with the enemy without sympathizing with the enemy. The ones who could do it were spies, the real thing. They were cold, very cold. He looked over at her as she sat there in her chair, the blond hair, the gray eyes, the beautiful mouth, the sleek body, and he knew in his heart there was only one reason a woman of her age would make the effort to be as attractive as that. So, which was she, spy or advisor? If she was as cold as he suspected, she would do her job and get the information so that the Agency could deport this guy. But if she was not, she would sympathize with this enemy she was wooing and might even come to love him.

"Well, dear," put in Maggie, "I have to say, if we're not spies, we're being used as spies. The Agency approached us through Richard, tested us, and swore us in. We certainly have been treated like employees, as far as what is expected of us, except that we're not paid. And we give up a lot, you know we do, dear. But look at the thing, we all sacrifice so much of our time, evenings, days when we can, even whole nights sometimes. And the sheer mental energy we put into following people, contacting them, developing a relationship with them, is beyond measurement. And all of it, to confirm suspected people. We may not record them, but we harvest a considerable amount of information. I mean, face it, we work very hard at this. I know we like to do it, but it is hard work, and I'm sorry, but I think it is dangerous sometimes. I admit, the Agency steers us away from danger. But they'll never shroud us completely. I don't know about Mr. Osipov, but some of these characters have been a threat to at least somebody."

Gretchin's chin went up. "You're saying, they're dangerous."

Maggie looked at her for a moment. "What I am saying, to all of us, is that the Agency calls us advisors but uses us as spies—volunteer spies, but spies, nevertheless. And as far as having the coldness for it, we *do*, I think, but to a limit, that's all. I think we should admit what we are. We get into people's lives and spy for information, usually against them. Maybe the work isn't terribly sinister, but I think it involves more spying than advising."

"I agree," returned Gretchin, nodding, "I totally agree. And I think it's a lot more dangerous than we've suspected. Shit, I sure don't want to have to start carrying a gun."

"The truth," Maggie added, turning to Martina, "is healthier, dear." And when there was no reply, "Right, then. How should we proceed with this Mr. Osipov? Everything as usual?"

Martina gave an affirmative nod. "As usual, yes. . . . I'll take the lead."

Gretchin pushed a handfull of hair behind an ear. "Would it be all right to talk to him on our own?"

Searching the aqua eyes briefly, Martina replied, "Of course, within reasonable limits."

"Sure."

There was a silence, and then Martina said, "All right. So, I think we're finished for tonight. I'll try to lead Mr. Osipov around for awhile and find out what more I can. If I get some information I'm not sure about, I'll text or email you and you can research it, all as usual. So, thanks for coming this evening. It's been interesting. Stick close to your phones and watch your email. Thanks."

After emptying the kettle, Maggie filled it for two cups and placed it on the burner. For her, making tea, even herb tea, was a ritual necessary for emotional equilibrium, and drinking the tea properly, that is, in an atmosphere conducive to its appreciation, formed part of her everyday thinking. Opening the tea cupboard, she sighed with pleasure at the neatness of its interior. The boxes and tins of tea, bags of coffee, packages of sugar, even the related whatnot stuff, lay stacked and lined up in logical order. Here even the blind could find what they wanted, for everything was where it made sense to be. How she wished she could configure the larger world so that she herself could be where it made sense to be, where even the blind could find her.

"They're gone," said Martina, setting the tray on the countertop. "We could be a really good team, but we fight ourselves, don't we? I think, you and I are the only two in the group who don't despise each other."

"Chamomile okay?"

Taking a seat at the table. "None for me, thanks. What's wrong?"

"I'm fine. You?"

"Of course. What's not to be fine with?"

"Well, I was thinking, Mr. Osipov, for one thing, and maybe Gretchin, for another."

"He'll be okay around Gretchin."

"I hate to be crude, dear, but she's got more than a smidgen of whore in her, you know. And you're not worried?"

"She heard me, Maggie. I was clear."

"Yes, you were."

Getting up and pushing the chair in, "I'm tired. Good night, Maggie. Sweet dreams."

And what else was there to say, she thought as she climbed the stairs. You wish the sweetest of dreams for the people you love, but you know that you're just wishing and that you can't make it so. And what would her own dreams be tonight? All her life, she had pursued the great ideas of humanity—truth, honor, justice. She had defended those ideas even when they were not entirely attainable. None of those ideas had ever pursued her. Now she had encountered another of the great ideas of humanity, the idea of love, and this time the idea had pursued her, as though it considered her to be defendable even if not entirely attainable. Was she attainable? Who in God's world knew? Perhaps she was not. But then, as she closed her bedroom door, just then, as she shut herself in, something, perhaps a voice, from the deepest part of her told her not to worry, that she had indeed been attained.

In her bed she opened her phone and called him. She waited for his voice and then spoke softly, as if directly into his ear, not saying hello, but simply, "Hi."

"Hi, yourself," he returned.

"I need to hear your voice."

"And I need to hear yours."

"Are we saying anything important, Stanley, could you tell me?"

"There is no way for me to do that. The power to know that is beyond me, I am sorry. But we are speaking, and we are listening, and that is what we want, yes?"

"Yes," she whispered.

"How did the meeting go?"

Sighing to herself, she replied, "You know, I love you, Stanley."

"Yes, I know this."

"How do you know? Maybe I don't love you. Maybe there's no such thing, maybe it is nothing."

"People say, it is only chemistry, no magic, only just chemistry. Chemistry is easier to work with, I think. Magic is difficult to work with."

"Chemistry is more predictable, dependable."

"Love can be magic, or it can be chemistry. For me, it is both. Some people want love to be absolutely nothing. Governments and armies want it to be nothing, and that makes sense, since it is probably their biggest enemy."

"You sound like an anarchist."

"How is it possible? I pay the taxes, and the taxes go to make the government. I have never actually met a genuine anarchist. Governments, armies, agencies, they are not bad people usually, but they do not want to encounter magic. And how did it go with the meeting? Did you tell them?"

"No, I didn't," she replied. "It was not the right time."

"Are you certain?"

"Yes." And then she asked, "Are you sure you want to fall in love with someone as old as I am?"

At length, he answered, "Yes, I am sure."

"Are you attracted to older women?"

"Yes," he replied. "I am attracted to older women, younger women, all women, all ages. I think I am attracted to older women because I was always especially close to my mother."

"So, you are attracted to older women especially?" As the question left her lips, she loathed herself for asking it.

He answered frankly, "Yes. Yes, I am. But love is more than attraction. At least, I hope it is, I believe it is."

With her eyes shut tight, she spoke softly, but fiercely. "Actually, I asked because they told me before that you liked older women. It was part of the information I had about you. I guess I was just being a spy again. I'm sorry. I don't want to be a fetish, Stanley."

"You are not a fetish."

"I'm sorry," she said. "I guess I've been in spy mode too long."

"It does not matter."

"God, it does matter, Stanley. I don't want to love you through suspicion."

"Yes," he replied softly.

And with eyes still shut, she breathed, as if to close the matter forever, "Yes."

"I love you, Martina. You have not one idea how much I love you. But the thing has to be done. We have to tell them—soon. Hiding for very long will make it worse. They will not know what to think, if we hide ourselves too much longer."

"Yes," she whispered.

CHAPTER 8

On Sunday morning Martina awoke early. Pulling the covers above her head, she thought of him. He had texted her from the studio Saturday afternoon to suggest they attend Sunday church together and spend the day in the city. She had received the message while in a department store fitting room and had laughed aloud, quickly texting him back that she was trying on bras at the mall and that it was inappropriate for her to discuss church in the nude. Now, in the darkness under the covers, she filled her mind with his image and imagined that his hands were moving over her body.

Slipping from bed, she stood before the full-length wall mirror and looked at herself. She wanted to remove the nightshirt to assess the beauty of the body she would offer him, but she could not bring herself to lift the garment. "I do look sixty-eight," she whispered. "I do." Then, in a sudden terrifying moment, she saw herself as perishing, and she turned away.

Yes, all the exercising and efforts had kept her slim and tight, she considered as she went into the bathroom, but it had not kept her young. Nature had given her a man in her old age, a man to perish in front of. Why was nature so weirdly cruel? Why not at forty-eight or even fifty-eight; but good gracious God in heaven, at sixty-eight. How grossly wretched and cruel.

She showered and then began to choose her clothes for the day. From her window she looked down at the curbside place where he would park. If he didn't come, she would be left with an empty street and an empty life. Shuddering, she turned from the window as she had turned from the mirror, and continued dressing.

"What do you think," she queried when Maggie stood suddenly in the doorway.

"You don't wear tweed much."

Running a silver comb through her hair, Martina smiled.

"I like it," said Maggie, leaning against the doorframe.

"English?"

"Well, let's say, except for the straight blond hair and maybe the silver comb, you don't *look* like a Nazi."

The gray eyes twinkled. "Post," she teased back. "My thinking is post-era. So, English?"

"Very."

A frown. "But it doesn't go with the black coat. I just don't wear brown a lot."

"You'll be taking it off, what does it matter?"

But he rang then, so she grabbed the coat and went down to the door.

"There you are," he said. "I have been wishing for a beautiful day, and you have made it beautiful already."

"Oh, I believe you," she joked, stepping out and pulling the door closed, "just like I would believe a toad."

"That is perfect," he laughed, "you are from the Black Forest area, yes?"

"Never actually been there, thank you," she retorted playfully and got into the car.

It did not seem to be a morning for conversation, and throughout the service they spoke not once. They sang the hymns, listened to the sermon, and watched the subdued play of light from the stained-glass windows. Occasionally she would look down at his knee beside her, and he would look down at hers. Even after the service they did not speak, but walked to the restaurant like two dumb wraiths in the sunlight. It was not until they had ordered and sat waiting for lunch that any conversation seemed plausible.

Then she said mischievously, "Do you know you've been staring at my hair?"

"Yes? I am sorry. It is a bad thing."

"Of course, it is. This is a new suit."

He looked at the suit. "It is very gorgeous, I like it, it looks very good on you, and I noticed it in the church."

"Thank you. It is supposed to look English. Yes?"

"Well, yes, English, I think."

Her eyes became slits of gray. "But you're not sure?"

"I am sure," he insisted. "English it is."

"Tweed is English."

"I know this," he replied defensively. "I have photographed women in tweed clothes before. It looks very good on you."

"But you were staring at my hair," she iterated. "You seem to stare at my hair a lot."

Exaggerating a shrug, he grinned. "What am I to say? If a man stares at a woman's front or her rear or her legs, he stands condemned just for doing it, but her hair is totally safe to stare at. And *yours*—oh! I mean, only Germans have hair like that. It is amazing. So, who can condemn me?"

"But I wanted to look English for today," she complained, putting on a frown.

"Yes, of course," he nodded, "and you do, very English."

Ruefully, "Toads again, I think."

Across Rittenhouse Square they found a corner in a small café and shared a slice of pound cake and blew upon ceramic cups of English breakfast tea.

"So, this church is part of your assignment?" she asked.

He separated a corner from the slice. "This church was not the part, no. But to be part of some church was in the assignment, yes. Actually it was only a suggestion, but a strong one. And I think it was a good one, from their perspective."

"Who do you mean?"

"The directors."

She lifted her cup and blew softly across the surface of the tea, toward him. "What have you found there? Because, I noticed you seemed to enjoy it."

He shook his head. "I am not certain. I think, mainly I have found the sense of quietness of some kind. The people are very nice."

"They seemed to be, yes." Carefully she tested then sipped her tea, searching his eyes. "You can't be going for the social part, though."

"Why not? The social part is good, it is the good part of life."

She shrugged. "You haven't struck me as someone who would need a social life. And why choose something so foreign, if you did?"

"Church? Oh, it is not so foreign for me. The churches in Russia are beautiful places, they are wonderful. You will love them when you see them."

"But the Christian thing, it seems foreign to your life."

He blinked playfully. "Really? Is this true, you think so? Stravinsky loved it." But when her eyes told him she thought his example lame, he grew serious. "I do not really know what to say about this. I do not have what those people have, I know this, but maybe I will at some time in my life, yes?"

She gave a simple nod of assent.

Then he asked, "Do you want to go with me to the church?"

Deliberately she lifted the cup, sipped from it, then put it down. "I suppose that might work."

"You are smiling," he said. "Why?"

"I was just thinking, your eyes are the most beautiful blue."

And when he dropped his gaze she looked at him as she had not done before. The fingers gripping the saucer and cup, the candid expression, the glasses, the striped collar, the heavy sweater, the arm of the leather jacket he had draped over his chair, all of it formed an image of loneliness and melancholy. But in spite of this, she could not pity him, but could only confirm that she loved him.

After a moment he looked up at her. "I cannot tell you how important I consider you to be, it is not possible. It is like you are some world, some whole world, all alone yourself, and I want to come into you and live in you."

With the lightest touch, she ran a finger across the back of his hand. "Listen, Stanley. I think we should talk about us . . . and about them, about all of it."

He leaned back against the jacket. "Yes, we do need to do that. I agree. Too much is involved. The future will not be happy on its own. We are stupid to think it will be happy on its own. We both are working for the dangerous people. They are very dangerous."

"Governments," she replied, matching his solemnity, "are always dangerous."

"I know this."

"But again, I think we should not tell each other any more than we have already about the people we work for. Not now, anyway. Someday, but definitely not now, yes?"

Nodding vigorously, "I agree," he said. "Yes, it is very wise, good."

Then he lifted his cup, sipped the tea, and looked at her, as if she was his muse. She was nude, and the platinum hair fell sleekly around her face. Sixteen hundred ISO, he thought, but no faster, and a short zoom, very fast. She was not moving at all, but was simply posing and breathing. It was perfect, the hair, the face, the shoulders, the breasts, all in a subdued light. It was gorgeous, just simply gorgeous.

"Do you know how you're looking at me right now?" she asked suddenly. When he did not respond she said, "Let's just say, I feel a little naked, Mr. Osipov."

"Nude, yes," he replied, "I am thinking of you nude."

"And I suppose you've got your camera."

"Yes."

Outside the café, they pulled their collars closed against the cold and waited for the Locust Street traffic to turn at their corner to begin making its way around Rittenhouse Square.

"And now," she said, giving her coat a final tug, "let's walk. Let's just walk a little."

Not far from the café they bought baguettes and coffee. Clutching the warm cups, they began to walk the perimeter of the Square. They did not hurry; why should they, for it seemed that time had stood still for them to fall in love. Savoring morsels of bread with sips of coffee, they strolled along as lovers, but lovers in a kind of gloom.

At the corner of 18th and Walnut they entered the Square and walked to its center. Everything seemed to have a grayness, a lonesomeness to it.

Near the empty wishing pond they stopped to finish their coffee and toss baguette crumbs to the pigeons. For a moment, they stood in silence, as if to withdraw from the world, with its friends, its lovers, its lives, its mechanisms, its powers, as it moved past them.

"You know," she said soberly, "we will be seen as traitors, it's really that simple. How could we not be?"

"We have already talked about this."

"I want to talk about it again."

"But look at it such as this," he suggested. "We have not betrayed them, we have forsaken them. I think there is a difference, yes?"

"Idealists always seem to think everybody else sees the distinctions they do." But he only looked down at his shoes, so she continued, more gravity in her tone, "We *told* each other. For them, that's betrayal enough."

"But we had to tell each other some of it. That is always what comes with loving someone. And we have talked about this before."

"I know that," she replied impatiently, "I just want to keep putting things on the table to look at them in full view, no deceptions, no tricks. What we're doing, have done, is very serious. It's a serious thing, and it shouldn't be something stupid."

"Yes, I am sorry, but love, I am thinking, is always stupid, yes?"

But suddenly he seemed somehow foolish and vulnerable, so that she had to look away from him. Then she said cheerily, "There are so many dogs here, it's like a kennel."

He beamed with appreciation. "It is a haven for dogs, as they say."

"You really enjoy those idioms, don't you?"

"Yes, of course," he grinned. "That was also part of my assignment, to be cool. But I am not supposed to be cool too much. I am only supposed to be a little cool."

"I don't know," she returned, "*Haven for dogs* is probably considered no cooler than *as they say*, so you might want to revise your list."

It felt good to laugh, and they began to enjoy the swarming of pigeons that had come in search of crumbs. They were laughing, the pigeons were fluttering and pecking, and gradually everything began to look less gray.

Then he said, "I would like to know something, so you must tell me, why did the Jungs name their daughter *Martina*?" And when her eyebrows rose he added, "Ah, you are surprised at my question, good. That means, there must be a story to tell. I like stories, so I am listening."

"Well," she replied, "let's see, actually, my parents liked Mussolini, do you believe it?"

"The fascist, the man with the marble chin."

"Both my parents were serious Germans. Actually they were believers, Nazis."

"Ooh, very bad. Do not tell anybody in this country. They will never understand Europeans. They are crazy over here."

"*I* am *over here*, I'll have you know. I'm an American, and I'm not crazy, so watch that."

"Okay, teacher. So, tell me the story, please."

She sighed. "My parents were not anti-Semitic or blood-thirsty or any of the other things, but they were both in the Nazi Party. They were extreme, quite extreme, I think. I suppose all Nazis were that. My father especially was a dedicated, extreme nationalist. He was so, *so* German."

"Yes, I understand," he smiled. "I am Russian, you do remember this, yes?"

"He was so incredibly German, I cannot tell you how German he was. When the Nazis came to power he said they were the best future for Germany and embraced them, but of course, he was naive and did not know anything about the whole picture. We lived in the countryside, so, what would you expect? He was really occupied with the past, or really just his ideas about the past. When he talked about the future he would always refer to the past, so it was like his whole state of mind was set in the past and projected into the future. Anyway, he believed in the old Germany, whatever that was, and for him, the Nazis seemed to give him hope again. Clearly, he was just a romantic. He was an intelligent man, but yes, a romantic. I think, actually, the Nazis were more or less just incidental. Anyway, I was born in August, about two weeks before we invaded Poland. Miraculously my parents, all of us, survived the war. I think we lived through it because of my father's work. We lived in a rural area during most of the war, and my parents even continued to have children. My father loved Italy—of course, a romantic, right? My mother was very fond of Italy, but my father adored it, absolutely adored it. Italy was second to Germany, for him, but both lay at the center of a very flat world. He loved Italy's sunshine, its art, its people, even its politics. He was a German of Germans, but I think, if he loved Germany, he was *in love* with Italy. He saw the relationship between the two countries as a great love affair, a marriage. Germany was the strong, warrior man, and Italy, the sensual woman. Yes, my father was quite romantic. His love for Italy continued, even after the war, and we actually vacationed there, I am not certain where, probably near Como, but it was very beautiful."

"Yes," he agreed, "it is beautiful, Como, the town, the lake, all of it is wonderful to look at."

"You've been there?"

"No, but I have seen many pictures. Photographers love that place. But it is said that you must go to the south for more sunlight, Rome and the small towns on the coast."

"Yes, that's right, I know, but my father said Italy was more civilized in the north. He said he liked the result of perspiration, not the smell of it. But he loved Italy, the whole idea of it. He used to say that France had many art museums, but that Italy *was* an art museum."

"I have a question," he said at length, "about your parents. What wish do you think they would want to see granted, *fulfilled*?"

She looked at him curiously. "That's an interesting question, my Mr. Osipov. I've never been asked anything like that before."

He shrugged, watching the pigeons.

"Do you mean, something they wished for before or after the war?"

He shrugged again. "It does not matter. But it is hypothetical, you know, not an actual wish."

"No, I understand. Well, I suppose, for my father, before the war he would have wished for Germany to flourish and be recognized as the true seat of truth in the world. Something like that."

"That is a very big wish."

She nodded solemnly. "But I think he also would have wished very hard for Italy to become part of Germany, for the two countries to be married, with Germany as the recognized center of truth, and Italy as the recognized center of beauty."

"And Austria?"

"He saw Austria as part of Germany, of course."

"Of course. And Austria would be the world center of what?"

"Music, obviously. But again, as part of Germany."

He rolled his eyes. "Of course."

"Remember, for my father, it was *a very flat world*. He was not a realist."

"And what about the wish of your mother, what would that have been?"

"I suppose, to have her family flourish, and also that when she became old my father would still see her as a woman the way she knew he would always see Italy as a country."

"So, your father did see her that way, before the war?"

"I think he always did, yes. But after the war, he was confused. He was damaged, really, and very confused."

"Not a man who survives?"

"No. He saved us so that we could survive, that was very important to him, but no, he was not one to struggle for his own survival. As I remember him after the war, I think he would have wished for some kind of reunification for Germany. When my mother became ill, he certainly would have wished for her health, the medicine she needed. But he was very confused about Germany, about the world, about life itself. The brutality of the war, the little that he saw of it or found out about later, crushed him and left him without a real sense of survival. He was too sensitive, he was a romantic."

"And your mother?"

"After the war, she would have wished for her health, so she could take care of her family and also be a lover to my father, be his Italy. But the truth is, I think, that if she was dying, he had already died inside. She must have known that. It was all quite hopeless—it usually is, for romantics. Life is brutal. It is for the realists. Idealists and romantics do not survive."

"Yes."

"When she died he seemed to die even more. Maybe he had no wishes, at all."

"That is very sad."

She looked at him. "And you are not sad, my Mr. Osipov?"

Dropping his gaze, he replied, "I do not know what I am, sad, happy, I do not know." Then he looked up, into her intense eyes. "So, you and your sisters all have Italian names."

She nodded, watching as he crumbled and tossed pieces of bread to the pigeons. One of the birds, pecking up crumbs from the cold pavement, worked its way closer to them until it stood and simply looked up at them with one eye.

"Memories are powerful," he muttered, releasing a few crumbs.

She shook her head slowly. "Memories save us, and they kill us, don't they?"

"That is exactly right, yes."

Then, for some reason, she seemed to need oxygen and drew a deep breath. The bare limbs of the surrounding trees made her feel suddenly colder, and she pulled the front of her coat closer around her neck. "I would ask about *your* name," she said, "but actually, it sounds quite normal."

"Yes, normal," he laughed. "*Stanislav*—do you like it?"

She chuckled, "We're children, right, and I'm going to say no?"

"Of course."

She held her eyes closed and then opened them. "Yes, I like it very much."

He shrugged, breaking off more crumbs for the pigeons. "I was born in Moscow, and my parents were very Russian, like I told you before. They were people of the city, metropolitan. I always wanted to live in the country and to have the many dogs." He laughed nervously, "What should I say?"

"Just tell me whatever you like, it doesn't matter."

"*Whatever you like*," he repeated, grinning. "You are not making a demand upon me, yes? I feel very secure, because of this."

"Oh. So, you feel secure, Mr. Osipov?" she teased. "Wait, let me turn my recorder on."

Melodramatically he put his hand to his forehead. "Yes, you are becoming CIA again. No, do not do it. And if you tell jokes like that, I will get nightmares. But listen to me, you are cold. Why not go back inside, and we can get more tea, yes?"

"I'm a little chilly, but I don't want to be heard. It's just better out here, but let's walk, I think that will help."

Taking her arm in his, he pulled her close to warm her, and accompanied by the soft flutter of scattering pigeons, they began to walk.

"Of course, it's warm in my bed," she said at length, "and very private, I could always invite you there. But I think I love you too much to do that."

"Yes," he said, speaking softly into her hair.

And then she said, "So, Mr. Osipov, please continue."

"The recorder is off?" he queried, with a grin.

"Yes, it is off."

"You are not CIA?"

"No," she replied softly.

"Yes, okay. So. My father liked fishing and hunting and of course, war. He was very happy with every East-West clash that happened. And it could be anything—U2, Cuba, Viet Nam—he loved it. He had a war brain, you know, like Patton, not just military, but war. He even kept score. My brothers and I would ask him who was winning, Russia or America, just to joke with him, but he would become very serious and actually start reciting from his scoring list he kept in his mind. I do not need to say, he loved the Cold War and only wished every day that it would turn hot. But he saw the changes coming, ideas changing. You have no idea how much he hated people like Gorbachev. He would always remind us, shaking his finger in warning, that Gorbachev was the only Soviet leader that was born after the Revolution."

"True?"

He nodded, and spoke into her hair again, nearly tasting it, "Oh, yes, very true. Do you consider that we are being listened to out here? It is chilly, you said, and I am just thinking that somewhere else would be warm and private."

"I know what you're getting at. No, no—no bed. Just talk, please."

"Okay, so. My father—what more is there for me to say? He loved vodka. He loved my mother and he loved vodka. He died in his sixties from liver disease. My mother is eighty and lives in Moscow. She was a musician and was always playing the piano at home. My father would make a joke that she was the degenerate one. Music was my mother's politics, and I think she played the piano as her way of expounding her views. When I was young she was strong and had a love of life. She respected her husband and loved her sons. Still, today, she is beautiful and sensitive. Her blond hair has turned to white, her eyes are still pale ice-blue, her skin is unspotted. She has the arthritis in her hands and no longer plays the piano."

"Do you miss her?"

"Yes," he replied simply, looking up into the sky.

Wishing she could look into his eyes, she said, "You're very much like her, aren't you?"

"Well, of course, I am, yes. But I am like my father too. My father smoked cigarettes, but like my mother, I never smoked. My mother would not drink my father's vodka, or any alcohol, but I drink scotch. So, I suppose, I became an artist and photographer for my mother Aglaya, and served the KGB and the government for my father Aleksey. I am a little, or perhaps much, of both of them, I think, yes." He looked at her. "Yes? Does that make sense to you?"

Gently she pulled herself closer to him as they walked. They were silent for a moment as other pigeons flew across their path and then settled onto the pavement.

"Pigeons," she observed, "are always waving, aren't they? Sometimes it's a welcome, sometimes a goodbye. And sometimes they just seem to be waving as you're passing through."

"They are sensitive," he chuckled. "A pigeon is a symbol of peace."

"You know," she said, "historically, Germans hate Russians, and Russians hate Germans. Capitalists hate Socialists, and Socialists hate Capitalists. So, from a historical perspective, you and I are supposed to hate each other."

"I am thinking," he replied, "that is a torch I do not want to carry."

"Or pass along to someone else?"

"Yes, you are correct, I do not want to carry it or pass it to someone else."

"Those are my thoughts exactly, Mr. Osipov."

"Good," he returned. "Then we are on the same page, as they say."

In the late evening, sitting in bed in her robe, she read the text that had just come through: *I miss you.* She could still feel his arm pulling her into him to keep her warm as they walked the Square. She replied with, *Good time. Thanks. I love R Square.* Then with a sigh, she closed the phone and waited. When it chimed she opened it again and read aloud, *"Rittenhouse or Red?"* Quickly she replied with, *Perhaps both. Good night.* Closing the phone, she held it between her hands and in her mind pressed her lips to his. It had been the beautiful day he had wished for.

Then she got up, laid the robe aside, and got back into bed. As she turned out the light she doubted that sleep would come easily. There was too much to think about, too much to do, and trading activity for sleep had never seemed a fair deal. Yes, it had been a lovely day, filled with the joys of being in love. But it had also been a day of consideration of dilemma. The governments they were forsaking were both willful and mighty and had left in their wakes innumerable dead. Only a fool would expect the minds behind those forces to understand and thus legitimize the forsaking of duty in favor of romantic love.

Closing her eyes, she thought of this Russian man she had fallen in love with, as he might be beside her now, kissing her, touching her. But he was not beside her, and it was not a time for touching, but for wishing, and what she wished for was more time in this world so that she might possess this man and he might possess her.

CHAPTER 9

She awoke cold. Hugging herself, she pictured him as there beside her, to warm her so that she would not have to warm herself. Quickly she reached above the covers for her robe, pulled it around her shoulders, and got out of bed.

An hour later, she wheeled into a corner spot of the school parking lot and shut the engine down. She watched in silence as Maggie closed her briefcase and pulled her gloves on.

"Do you feel that heat?" she asked, clearly annoyed. "The car is off and it's still warm in here."

"It wasn't that cold, dear," Maggie returned defensively. "I always set it for sixty-four at night. I just wanted to try sixty-two once, just once."

"Good God, Maggie, you're the one who hates the cold, you can't stand it, you've said that a thousand times."

"Don't complain. Everyone is supposed to be more *green*. We should all try to be environmentally sensitive."

"Green, not blue, Maggie. I couldn't even take a shower, it was so cold in the bathroom."

"I was cold myself, dear. But trust me, if we don't do something to save the ozone, we'll burn at the beach. Don't complain, buy an electric blanket or get a man."

"Electric blankets are not environmentally sensitive, you should know that."

"I suppose, a man would be greener than an electric blanket."

"My lips were blue in the bathroom mirror."

A relenting sigh. "All right, dear, no more sixty-two. Let's go in, I'm getting cold."

Martina dropped the keys into her purse with a clink of exasperation and opened her door.

During the lunch period she went to her classroom and closed the door. She took her seat at the old desk and looked up at the clock. Since the student body had been dismissed at noon and most of the teachers were now gone, the atmosphere in the school, especially in her classroom, seemed strange, ethereal. After taking a moment to smile into the face of the clock, she opened her phone and called him.

"Stanley?"

"Hi, Martina."

"I just wanted to hear your voice."

"I was going to text you, actually," he replied. "My contact called me today."

"What does that mean?"

"She wants to see me."

"Why?"

"I have not a single idea, Martina. I am not due to see her, but they are pretty good at knowing things about their people. Sometimes they are watching me, I know this. I am certain your people do this same thing."

"Probably."

"Russians are very good at interpreting behavior. I do not know, but maybe they have been watching me."

"What did she say?"

"She asked me the usual questions, how things were going, whether I was socializing at the church, if I had met any individuals, the usual things. But then she said she wanted to visit me, to have a talk. I am not perfectly certain, but I think she is suspicious about me. It was her tone. I am Russian and I can interpret behavior, too, and there *was* suspicion in her voice."

She did not reply, but then, "Listen, come over tonight, after dinner. We have to talk."

"What about Maggie? We should always be talking in secret. I do not think I am happy to trust anybody."

"She's going out tonight. Come over about seven."

In a tweed jacket and jeans, he sat with her on the front room couch and watched as she poured their tea. There were cookies and fruit and broccoli with dip, and his eyes followed the movements of her body as she prepared a little plate and then handed it to him. She said the tea had been steeping and should be very strong, like Russian tea. Although it was English tea, it should remind him of Russia. If he didn't care for it, she would be surprised. As he had watched her body, he listened to her voice.

"You have to close your eyes," she said, "to really taste this tea. Don't argue with me, now, just close your eyes and go on."

He obeyed, sipping the hot tea with his eyes closed. "It is very strong, yes, and very good. In Russia, it is said that the strong tea will get you through the cold winter. But look," he said, displaying the sleeve of his jacket, "I am English, what do you think?"

"Well," she laughed doubtfully, "I am not convinced, Mr. *Osipov.*"

"Yes, I understand, but also, you are the most German-looking woman I have ever seen. You do not look English, either, and you do not look American, you look *so much* German. You are very beautiful." His eyes followed the platinum hair down to the black sweater. In his career as a photographer he had never been comfortable thinking of women as objects from which to produce images, but this woman was more than simply a person. This woman was a thing as well as a person, a what as well as a who, a kind of organic idol. "Before we talk," he said softly, "can I touch you?"

Carefully he set his cup on the tray, took hers and did the same, and then leaned toward her and kissed her lips gently, as though he kissed a cloud. When their lips parted, he brought his hand to her shoulder and then tenderly followed the curves of her sweater down to her waist. She did not resist.

"I am touching you," he said.

"Yes," she whispered.

"But I am not exploring. I am touching you with reverence."

"I know."

Then he kissed her again, this time longer and less delicately. "I am sorry that I am a man and want to touch all of you."

"Don't be sorry," she replied. "I want to touch you." Then he sat back and looked away, as if confused, and she reached for his tea and placed the cup in his hand again. "But now," she said seriously, "we have to talk."

"You are the thinking woman. What are you thinking?"

"That maybe we should just tell them." And wishing she could dive into the blue of his eyes, she added, "I don't think either side would try to hurt us."

But as if he had not heard her, he said, "I like these cookies," and then bit into one and chewed slowly.

"Yes, I know you do. But you are thin."

"We are both thin. I like pastry too."

Humoring him, she said, "Well, don't like it too much, Mr. Osipov, it's not good for you."

"Like love?"

She only nodded her affirmation.

But then he said seriously, "I agree, I do not think they will hurt us. We should not be worth it to them."

Watching as he sipped his tea, she said, "But they can arrest us and detain us for a long time. We have to be realistic, both sides have an interest, and neither side is friendly."

He looked away from her then. "Where would your people put you?"

"The Agency? God knows. They're capable of anything, absolutely anything. And of course, they have just about every means at their disposal. But it doesn't matter, it really doesn't. You would not be there, ever again. What about your people?"

"Well, as they say here, you have to be kidding. They will do what they want, it is very simple. I can be arrested, taken back to Russia, or just shot. Who would protest? My mother? My brothers? Who would even know about it? The Russians will do what they want. If either side wants to separate us, it will happen, we will not see each other again. My people would even collaborate with your people to do it. And the reality thing is, if they do *anything* to us, if they take any action whatever against us, we are lost."

"That would separate us, wouldn't it?" When he did not reply she said, "We're not spies."

"We are *like* the spies. To a government, we are spies. And a spy cannot marry a spy from the opposite side."

She smiled. "We're too old, aren't we?"

"Too old? I do not understand."

"We're too old to wait anything out, like a prison term."

"Yes, we are too old for that," he agreed, gazing into her eyes. Then he said, "So. You want to tell them. What do you propose?"

She nodded thoughtfully. "Actually," she said at length, "I propose marriage. That's what I propose."

He brought the cup again to his lips.

"Yes," she continued, "why not? What else is there, suicide, an armed stand?"

"Ridiculous."

"Exactly. But if we marry publicly and then simply tell them privately, but together, that we're leaving them to live our lives together, they, both sides, might just let it go."

At length he said, "I have nothing of myself to propose. I think, it sounds like we should try it."

"So, are you proposing?"

"No," he answered soundly, "I am *accepting*. I accept your proposal, with all of my heart."

She leaned closer, kissed him lightly upon the lips, and then said, "Here's to our survival." And she kissed him again, not lightly, but deeply, and then sat back to look at him. When she reached to take his hand, to pull him to her, the front door latch clicked and Maggie came in.

"Hi, you two," she sputtered, shuddering from the cold. "Oh, I hate the winter. Sometimes I think nature has no compassion whatever, something is having fun making me cold." And reaching for the top button of her coat, she quickly added, "Yes, I know what you're going to say, dear. Don't worry, I'll leave the heat up tonight."

Martina patted a cushion. "Come and have something hot, Maggie?"

"No, I'm on my way up to bed, thank you, I'll just say goodnight, dear. And goodnight, Stanley."

He raised a hand. "Goodnight, Maggie."

They were silent until she had gone, then he said it was late and he should leave, and she reached to touch his hand. She went to the closet and before he left she pulled the front of his coat closed, kissed his cheek, and told him to stay warm. When he asked helplessly how that was done, she returned his helpless look, then opened the door and pushed him out into the winter night. She waited until he had gotten into his car, then she closed the door, for she did not want to see him drive away.

Maggie, already in her robe, seemed to be waiting for her on the landing. Choosing not to meet the green eyes, Martina asked, "How does one get through life, Maggie?"

"You're asking the wrong person, dear."

It was an hour later that Maggie knocked at the door and opened it. She stood looking at her friend, as if at a broken icon.

"Yes?" Martina asked patiently from her bed, gently patting the towel that turbaned her wet hair.

"I just wanted to say that I know. It probably won't help, but I know."

"What do you know?"

"You are pretending, dear."

"Pretending what?"

"That you haven't fallen in love with him."

"What are you talking about?"

Maggie shook her head. "Good Lord, why do humans lie. You're not doing the math, dear, if you think I don't know. Twenty years, and you think I don't know? That's quite an insult."

Moistening her lips, Martina made no reply. She continued nervously to pat the towel as Maggie came to sit on the bed. She determined not to give in, but to remain silent, to remain stalwart. She would admit to nothing. But then, inexplicably, as if the stars had somehow realigned themselves, releasing her, opening for her a window to see through and a door to walk through, she felt herself go limp inside and heard her own voice declaring, "Yes. Yes, I love him, Maggie. I'm sorry, yes, I love him." And then the tears came, and she could not stop them.

Maggie shook her head slowly.

"You were right, Maggie. I'm sorry for lying to you. He loves me, Maggie, he does. I've been trying to keep it secret, because I was afraid, desperately afraid."

"I think this is very serious, Martina. I would be afraid, too. It's just very serious. Do you know how serious this is?"

Pressing the edge of the sheet to her eyes, Martina moaned. "Actually, I do, Maggie."

Staring fearfully, Maggie queried, "You didn't tell him, did you?"

"I did."

"Oh God, oh please, Martina, why did you do that?"

"Because he told me his side, he confessed to me, without knowing who I was. He was doing the whole thing. He was here to become an American for the Russians. He told me everything. He just came out with it and told me."

"Are you certain he didn't suspect you? He could have been planting information, dear."

Removing the towel from her head, Martina looked into the green eyes. "He was not planting, Maggie. I would have known. He was actually shocked when I told him later what I was, and I would have known if he was faking. I've got that sense of things, Maggie, you know I do. Even Richard knows I do. I can sense the slightest deception, and I certainly know when someone is lying. Stanley was not faking. I've never been wrong, Maggie, not one time, not one single time."

Maggie rolled her eyes. "I know, that's true. And not this time, not the slimmest chance of it?"

"No."

"Do you know what you're going to do?"

"Maggie, we love each other. We're leaving the programs."

"That's ridiculous."

"I suppose it is."

"And his political sympathies are what?"

The answer came with effort. "He's a Marxist."

"Well, this is wonderful, just wonderful. So, you escape Communist East Germany, come to America, and fall in love with a Russian Marxist. I mean, is that completely stupid, or what? It's ludicrous."

"Maggie, neither of us cares anymore. He has his opinion, I have mine. Sometimes they match, sometimes not, but we don't want to be part of the struggle."

"The struggle?"

"The struggle for dominance of ideologies. Look, he is more a socialist than I am, that's all."

"I should hope so, dear."

"Yes, but, so what? You know, I think all I'm saying is that we fell in love with each other. We didn't ask for it to happen, Maggie."

"God, how many times have I heard something like that."

"So, what are you saying, Maggie? What exactly would you have us do?"

"It really doesn't matter what I think. It does matter what Richard and his people think. To them, Mr. Osipov is an infiltrator."

"Yes, well, maybe a little candor would be good, Maggie. We all know the Americans have been infiltrating Russian society for years, everybody with a brain knows that."

"Immaterial, dear. To the Agency, he's a spy."

Martina pointed to herself. "In this situation, I'm certainly as much a spy as he is."

"That doesn't matter to the Agency, dear, and you know it. They don't moralize about anything, except body count. They don't care that you love each other. The people in the Agency love their country, not its enemies."

The gray eyes looked at the ceiling, then into the green eyes. "We are not continuing in our roles. We're leaving, we are both leaving."

"That might not matter, either. You've told each other about your programs, which makes you double agents. I mean, the Agency will assume you've told each other everything. I don't know what Richard is going to say, I really don't. He's not a fake bastard, dear, he's a real one, and he just might see you as a traitor, certainly a criminal, since you were sworn to secrecy. Just how much did you tell him? Did you talk about the rest of the team?"

"Not specifically."

"I don't know, dear. You were sworn to secrecy. You are the team leader, for God's sake."

"I know. I know that. But I've also found the man I love."

"And that's what, exactly? What is this 'man-I-love' concept, except naive? What is he? What? The Hope Diamond? I mean, he's just a man, an organism, and a Marxist organism, at that."

"I am sixty-eight years old. I'm an old woman, you said it yourself. It's not just my last chance, it's the only chance I've had in my lifetime. I am in love with him, Maggie. I've never been married, never been in love. But this man fell in love with me, and I've fallen in love with him."

Steadying her gaze upon the gray eyes, Maggie asked, "And you don't care that he's a Communist?"

"No."

"How is that possible, dear? Communism killed your mother."

"I'm not so sure of that. I think people killed my mother."

"And you don't think ideologies make people what they are, even a little?"

"No. No, I don't. A lot of things have cleared for me."

"You're not worried that love is supposed to do just the opposite?"

"No, I'm not worried about it. This man, Maggie, is a good man. He's compassionate and loving and good. Very simply, he would not have refused my mother the help she needed, and he would not have broken my father's heart."

"So, you kiss, you consummate, and you wake up with a Communist in your bed. I love it. You know, it's hard enough for Democrats and Republicans to live together, a lot of couples just can't do it, but Marxists and Democratic Capitalists? Please. You exasperate me. Why should I need to tell you these things?"

"Maybe," replied Martina meekly, "because you're the history teacher."

"And you are the leader of a CIA advisory team, for God's sake. You're the one who escaped from East Germany. Your mother died there and your father gave up everything and risked his life and yours to get you out, and you want to marry back into it? Nothing could be more ludicrous."

Martina put her hands together. "Maggie, I have nothing to say, except that I don't care anymore about the struggle of the systems, whatever the systems were or are or ever will be."

"And what about his program, what about yours? The whole point of the CIA initiative is to thwart the Russian program to infiltrate American society. The Russians are actually doing it, Stanley Osipov is one of them. Do you really want the Russians here?"

"Sure, it's a good question."

"You're right, it is. And who do you want to carry it on when you leave? Do you want the rest of the team to just carry on as usual? And who do we catch, another Mr. Osipov? If we don't catch them, they'll be here in hordes—they're here now. Do you want the Russians here?"

The gray eyes blinked. "The answer is, yes, I want them here. I don't want the infiltrators here, but the Russian people *are* here, huge numbers of them, they have been here all along. I'm sure they're a vital part of American society, a beautiful part. I never saw that before. Yes, I do want them here. And I wish Americans could be part of Russian society, I wish the two countries could come to love each other, instead of hate each other."

"You sound like a child, an absolute child."

"The Russians," Martina replied resolutely, "are wonderful people, I have seen that in him. I love this man, Maggie, and I *am* going to go with him, and we *are* both going to walk away from all of it."

"Or at least, try."

"Yes, try."

"Where do you think you'll go, to a country that doesn't have politics or ideologies?"

Placing her hands on the sides of her head, as if to protect it from invasion, Martina replied, "Maggie, I don't know. I really don't know. But we'll find somewhere. Maybe here, or maybe Russia."

"Russia."

"Yes, Russia. Why not? I can't wait to go there, actually. I want to get to know his mother, his brothers, his whole family, I can't wait to meet them. And yes, I could live in Russia, very easily. Or we could live some other place, what does it matter? The point is, we love each other, and that's what our lives are going to be about from now on."

The green eyes looked away. "You're naive, dear."

"Yes, Maggie, I am. It's like I'm a child again. I have my youth again."

"You know, dear, you can drown in the fountain of youth."

Martina sighed. "If I do, will you pull my body out?"

The green eyes met the gray eyes again. "Yes, dear. Yes, I will." Then she arose to leave the room, but in the doorway turned briefly to say, "I think, we'll always be there for each other. Goodnight, dear."

"Goodnight, Maggie. Thank you."

Lifting the towel to fluff her hair, Martina thought of him, of his blue eyes, his gentle spirit. She tried to imagine living in Moscow and being part of his family. Then she put the towel down, reached for her phone, and accessed Sophia's number.

CHAPTER 10

When his cell phone rang on Tuesday evening he hesitated before accepting the call. He had been thinking of the pleasant dinner earlier with Martina and the warm atmosphere of the restaurant, in which they had joked, laughed, talked intimately, kissed. Reluctantly he put the instrument to his ear.

"Hello," he said.

"And how are things with you?"

This was what she always said to him, but now for some reason her voice seemed strange, weirdly foreign. It was odd, he thought, how nature had so configured the human voice that it nearly always revealed the character of the mind that employed it. A very cold wave passed over him, and he reached for a kitchen chair and sat before answering.

"Things are going well," he replied. "How are things with you?"

A low chuckle. "Any problems?"

"No," he answered, physically shaking his head. "No problems."

Momentarily she said, "I told you I wanted to see you."

"All right. You will come to my house?"

"No. Come to see me, at a friend's house tomorrow night. Can you come tomorrow night?"

"I think so."

"Not sure?" she queried, her tone iced with sarcasm.

"Yes, that would be fine."

"Good, it is settled. You will come at seven?"

"Fine."

"Take this down."

After writing the address he heard the connection die and closed the phone. Then he opened it again.

"Hi, Martina. We have to talk. She called again."

"She wants to see you?"

"Yes. Tomorrow night. What do you say?"

"I think we should tell them, both of us, right now, just like we said."

"Yes. Yes, I agree. All right, I will."

She pleaded, "Call me afterwards?"

"If I do not call you, I will call you when I get home."

"I'll want to know," she protested, "whether you're all right. Just text me, if you want, but let me know that you're okay."

"All right, I will, yes. Then I will call you when I get home."

"Yes. I'll wait. *Peace.*"

Softly he returned, "That is a strange word."

Then he went to the studio couch and sat where he had sat the first day. Imagining her beside him again, he relived that day, when she asked him to sit and then told him what he never could have imagined being so.

The next evening, precisely at seven, he extracted the key from the steering column and got out into the dark and the cold. The walkway to the house was short and he soon touched the button beside the mailbox, pressing it for a moment. Suddenly the inside door was cracked open enough to expose an eye, and then was opened fully. A woman with yellow hair opened the storm door, and he stepped past her into the choking stench of cigarette smoke. Turning to face her, he felt instantly repulsed by her unusually heavy makeup and utterly false smile. His repulsion was heightened when she spoke.

"Come in," she said in a rasping smoker's voice. Closing the door, she directed, in a heavy Russian accent, "Take a seat. There. On the sofa."

Across from him, she let herself fall into a stuffed chair upholstered in red vinyl, where she seemed to freeze into a kind of sinister motionlessness in order to look him over. Then, as if coming to life for a purpose, she again produced the smile, but only briefly, and asked, "Are you perfectly all right?"

"Yes," he replied, although he could not recall feeling more uncomfortable.

"Take your jacket off. Be comfortable. We are civilized, yes? Of course."

Awkwardly he slipped the jacket off and laid it beside him. The couch, the entire room, stank of tobacco smoke, and there seemed to be less oxygen in the air than he needed to speak without gulping. He could not resist the spectacle of the woman's grotesque makeup, her tasteless clothes—the sweater with its secondhand look, the polyester pants much too short, the shiny vinyl shoes. It seemed she had stuffed herself into all of it. Normally he would have thought her pathetic, but he could not have mustered pity here, for all the world.

Cautiously, he asked, "Where is—?"

"Your contact?"

"Yes."

"Talk to me, Mr. Osipov, just to me." Unconsciously she raised a plump hand and drew a tobacco-stained forefinger across her lower lip. Then, quite deliberately, as if the discovery of this action had made her uncomfortable, she lowered the hand and peered at him with small, inquisitive eyes, waiting for him to speak.

"But she called me," he said, "last night."

Her face cracking with a smile that was no longer merely false, but menacing, she said, "To *me,* Mr. Osipov."

He made no reply to this, his eyes traveling over the yellow hair piled up like dough.

"Who is the woman, Mr. Osipov?"

"What woman?"

"The woman you are dating at this time," she answered frigidly.

"Martina?"

She nodded. "Martina. Yes. Yes, Martina. You are dating her now, that is the truth. Who is Martina?"

"Martina Jung," candidly. "She is a school teacher."

"Ah, the German," she grunted with disgust. "Yes, Martina Jung, the German. You were seen with her."

"So, I am being watched. No bugs?"

"Bugs. Yes," she laughed. "Of course, no. There is no money for such things. That is why we are in this dirty country. The money is here, for right now."

"Dirty?" he repeated, incredulous.

Her eyes shrinking, she blurted, "No bugs. And beside this question, you are not important enough to be listened to." After he did not reply, she asked, "You are a photographer?"

He nodded, gulping for oxygen.

"Who bought the camera? Russia?"

"I did. I bought it. Actually, I have many cameras. But I am the one who bought them, yes. Why?"

"When I ask the question, I want to ask it. Do not ask *why*."

He shrugged indifferently, his gaze following her fat fingers as they crept ominously along the chair's arm. The chair had been poorly reupholstered, and a flap of its red vinyl material, stapled mercilessly, hung ready to come loose again. The rest of the furniture, like the woman's clothes, seemed oddly mismatched. The filthy shag carpet, the antiquated television set, the grimy lamp, sickened him somehow.

"You are in love with the woman?" she asked.

"Is that a charge or a question?" he returned.

She stared at him. "It is a question."

He hesitated, but then answered, "Yes. Yes, I am in love with her."

Grunting a raucous laugh, her belly heaving, she blustered, "And she is in love with you, that is how it works." When he merely shrugged at this, she shrugged back at him, as if to outdo him. Then her demeanor became suddenly grimly serious, and she pointed at him with her yellowed forefinger. Nearly drooling with viciousness, she slurred out, "We do not care. You are not important to us."

"I never thought I was," he replied weakly, recoiling from the sheer hatred in her demeanor.

She smiled gruesomely. "It does not matter much. You are in love with the German. So. It means nothing."

"If it does not matter, why am I here? Why did my contact call me to come here?"

"You are nothing to us," she repeated, more to make the fact than state it, her plastered face as emotionless as painted meat.

If only the fact was accurate, he thought. He had no choice but to accept her words at face value. Fate, as always, would speak the last words, anyway, and today, tomorrow, or whenever, either some people would come to shoot him or they would not. So many times he had tried to pin the future on intentions, such as those of this ludicrously deceptive and malignant woman, only to have fate step in at the end and deliver the final words like a closing soliloquy. Why did life always have to be so uncontrollable and thus so melancholy?

Then suddenly he said, "She knows about the program." And when her ghastly face seemed to lose all life he added, "I told her. I told her about the program."

For an extended moment the face remained fixed, as though embalmed. Then the burned voice asked, "How much did you tell the school teacher?"

"I did not tell her too many details, but I did tell her about me and about what the Russian program was supposed to achieve."

"So, what is this, it is garbage. It means nothing, I am not impressed."

"She is," he continued, "an advisor to the CIA."

Producing a great snort, she blabbered, "That is stupid. How do you know this?"

"She told me it was true."

"I am not impressed."

"I am not trying to impress you," he replied coolly. "They know about the program. The CIA knows about the Russian program." Then, in the grim silence that followed, he watched her macabre face as she fell into calculation.

At length she said, "So, of course they know this. We are aware of that they know this." And with her accent growing thicker, she said, "They can do nothing to us. They are impotent. They trip over each other, and they are chained by their laws. Democracy has put them in the prison. They are stupid and weak. They cannot do a single thing about us. If they report about us, Congress will laugh at them, they will laugh really loud and say, 'Another plot, ha!' They can do nothing to us."

"I did not say they could."

Now she nearly spat her anger, "Capitalists are always the same one thing. This country is a toilet."

"But of course, you know," he offered, "many people in Russia are Capitalists now."

Her eyes shrank to mere dots, but then suddenly grew to animated bulbs. Ejaculating a laugh, she boasted, her arms moving back and forth as if manipulating a steering wheel, "Yes. I have the Chevy, ha!"

"Chevy, really," he returned, suppressing a chuckle. "This is a significant possession."

The eyes became beady again. "It is rented."

"Maybe," he suggested flippantly, "you can get an option to buy."

"*And,*" she threw in, ignoring him, "I eat the hoagies!"

Observing the bulges in her sweater from her porky breasts, he replied, "I can see that."

She was silent for a moment, then blustered out, "I am making the decision. We do not need you anymore. I am releasing you right in this moment."

He looked at the plopped hair, the wretched face, the stretched sweater, the soiled pants, the shiny vinyl shoes. When he reached for his jacket she instantly pushed herself up out of her chair, grunting to seize the initiative, and stood over him, glowering fiercely. Only a few times in his life had he felt such intense malice from another's eyes. He stood, put the jacket on, connected the zipper, and pulled the tab up to his chest.

"Leave now," she commanded. "Do not come back." Then she stepped to the door, pulled it open, and repeated, "Leave now."

As he drove away through the quiet winter streets of Philadelphia's Greater Northeast he knew that he could expect never to see the woman or his regular contact again. Doubtless the house had been borrowed for the meeting, and tomorrow its owner, probably also Russian but not part of the program, would deny any knowledge of any of it. And that would be as it should be.

The traffic was heavy as he drove south on Roosevelt Boulevard, and he kept to the outer lane. At the Red Lion Road crossing he quickly texted Martina a simple *Okay*. When he reached Adams Avenue he parked in front of the home center and went inside, but did not take a cart. Methodically, without looking at the merchandise, he walked the first aisle, then the second, the third, and on, until he reached the rear corner of the building. After crossing the store, he entered the garden center and did the same thing. Then he left the store and finished the drive back to Olney.

In the studio, he stood by the couch where they had sat and talked. He wished he could make her appear, or even go and get her. But life was not like that, and wishing was futile. But if angels came and blessed them, gave them to each other, then he would ask her to sit on the couch and he would kneel before her. And with reverence he would touch and caress her body, kiss her body everywhere. But reality was not like that, and the angels would not be coming to bless them.

Catching up the D3, he slipped into its strap and then sat on the couch, beside her place. His style was to wear the strap across his body, slinging the camera under his arm, letting it ride on his hip, sometimes pushing it to ride at the center of his back. This arrangement allowed him to run or climb and yet keep the camera safe and ready to shoot. Invariably his colleagues considered a strap to be the mark of an amateur. An American photographer informed him that no pro would ever be caught dead using a strap, and that if he wanted to look seasoned he would do better to throw his away and just be willing to drop the frigging machine if he had to. He had wanted to reply that years of following the KGB on their murderous jaunts had instilled in him a sense that stupidly dropping his camera could result in a one-way trip to Siberia. But he had simply smiled at the advice and continued to use the strap. Gripping the hefty camera now, he switched it on and off, then stretched his legs out comfortably and put his head back. Then he reached for his phone and placed the call to hear her voice.

"Stanley?"

"Hi, Martina."

"What happened? Are you okay?"

"I am just fine, everything is good and okay, I think."

"But you're not sure?"

"No, I am not sure. My contact was not at the house where I went to meet her. I talked to somebody else, a much more important person. She is a very dangerous person."

"How dangerous?"

"I do not know. She is some top person, I think."

"GRU?"

"Sure, probably. I suppose she is GRU, but strictly field agent, I think, no desk job. She was like some dirty clown. I should have taken pictures."

"It would have been the last time you ever pressed a shutter release button, Mr. Osipov," she retorted.

"Yes, this is exactly correct," he laughed. "But she is too much filled with hatred to be a desk job person. I think she has the authority to order someone to be eliminated. She is a creepy clown, very scary."

"How did it go? And you can skip the imagery, Stanley, if you don't mind. Think, *pithy*."

"How did it go? Who knows this?"

"Meaning?"

"Anything you like it to be. It is impossible to know what she meant by what she said to me. She knew about you. I was watched. Russians are not suspicious of Russians for no reason. We were told that surveillance was part of the program, but I never saw it happening, I saw no one. So, anyway, I decided on the spot, as they say, to be honest. I told her about you, that you were working for the CIA."

"And?"

"Actually, she laughed at me."

"Genuinely?"

"I don't think so."

"She didn't ask more about me?"

"No, there was nothing. She said that I was not important to them, that I was not needed. She dismissed me, she released me from the program. But this could mean anything. They are always strategic, deceptive, like your people are, only more of what they are. Listen, can we go to dinner tomorrow evening, we will stay out late, yes? And I will tell you everything that happened."

"If you're still alive."

He laughed, "You are pessimistic."

"It's a dangerous world."

"It used to be *our* world. We are having no regrets, as they say, yes?"

"No regrets," she replied softly. "Yes, tomorrow night would be fine, let's do that. I'll look for you at five? You know, Stanley, I don't want to spend much more of my life without you."

"I know this," he replied. "Do you know where I am? I am sitting on the couch, where you told me to sit that day, but you are not here. I feel like I am a child, and I don't know what to do. I am sorry."

"Don't be," she returned. "I'm with you, we're together."

CHAPTER 11

Slowing the elliptical exerciser, Maggie took deep breaths. Then she switched the machine off and stepped to the floor to stretch and to normalize her heart rate. But she could take her time, for she had the evening to herself.

As she switched on the treadmill and began to walk, already the slideshow of the Bermuda pictures had begun on the basement screen. Keeping the treadmill's pace slow and its elevation at zero, she watched as the white beaches and aqua water drew her back to the vacation they had taken eight years before. Martina, always wary of what the sun might do to her skin, had only agreed to go with her following months of coaxing. They had splurged and stayed at the Princess. For two weeks that summer they lived and played as if all the island had been preserved for their pleasure alone. On sunny days, they explored beaches, frolicked in string bikinis, and swam in mild ocean water. In the late afternoons, they played tennis or shopped in Hamilton, always, it seemed, laughing in a kind of sweet euphoria. Once, when they had ventured out on motorbikes and returned too late to be served dinner at the Princess, they were forced to ride into town in search of a restaurant. There, two men vacationing from Melbourne, surely in their middle age and looking every bit like rich playboys, struck up a conversation with them and offered to give them a ride back to the Princess. But in spite of being flattered, they declined 'the offer of the playboys,' as they would come to refer to it, and rode back in the darkness on their own.

Her dark hair had been longer then, and although everyday during that vacation she let it go to the devil, still men looked at her, followed her with their eyes, wanted her. Martina, of course, her platinum hair a stunning flame against every background, they devoured with their eyes and wanted even more. But she was not jealous of Martina, had never been jealous of her. If Martina had been a friend or a sister, she might have envied her, competed with her, and perhaps even come to hate her in a womanly way. But Martina, exquisitely beautiful, possessed of noble dreams, was so very much more to her than a friend or a sister ever could be—she was a soul mate of soul mates to her. She could never compete with Martina, envy Martina, hate Martina.

At the final picture, she paused the player, switched off the treadmill, and stood looking at the album's final photograph. The Atlantic sky, dreamily blue and ethereal, the Bermuda sand, like crushed white glass, the shallow aqua waters running up to the beach, seemed to offer heaven in pictorial form. And at the picture's center, Martina, alive with the joy of freedom, posing like a glamour goddess in a black string bikini.

The Bermuda days were gone, Maggie thought, as a good phantom is gone when the dream is over. Now the present and the future seemed ominous, and she sensed the nearness of a precipice. As she climbed the basement stairs her watch showed ten minutes till eight. Martina and her Mr. Osipov, out to dinner, might even at that moment be looking into each other's eyes. They were to spend the evening together, no doubt to form their plans. Those plans, she considered, closing the basement door, might very well lead them all over the precipice.

They had requested a table in a corner, for its seclusion. The waiter, unhappy that the table's proximity to a window would cool the meal too quickly, protested melodramatically, but finally relented. He was still lamenting the situation when finally he served up the dinner.

"I am sorry," he moaned, setting the hot plates before them and wrinkling his nose at the obviously white window panes. "Look at this window, it is covered with frost. How can you expect to enjoy your meal? The other tables are warm, and if you'd like to change, it's no problem, and I can zap the steaks to keep them hot."

Their assurance of their contentment with the table only wrinkled his demeanor further, and he swayed with anxiety as he left to get their coffee. Upon his return, he could not refrain adding a final touch to his protest. "I hate to see such a lovely couple sit in a cold corner, but do what you want. If you get cold, just stick your feet in the coffee."

The table's single glowing candle, however, seemed more to set the mood than did the icy window. When the main course was finished and dessert had been served, they sat in their corner content, as if dreaming together, the light of the candle sparkling from their eyes.

It was then that she said softly, spontaneously, "Stanley, I love you."

"Yes," he replied, nodding, as if to acknowledge a fact. "And I love you."

"Does life go on forever?"

Shaking his head, he smiled. "It does not, and it should not. But of course, we know this, so, why do we ask the question? Why do we need to ask the question and to hear the answer? It is like we are lost and blind and can only shout to hear our voices from the walls to tell us where we are."

"Exactly," she agreed. "It's as if humans must rehearse their own sadness, their own sad end."

Her hair seemed to glow in the candlelight. He followed it down to the shoulders of the black-velvet dress, then lifted his coffee cup to his lips. It was not the first time that he had wondered why God had chosen to build the mind of Stanley Osipov to be so acutely sensitive to images in a physical world. An art teacher had once warned him to beware of images because they could kill an artist, they could slay his soul. But could they really, he had returned, or would not the danger come from within the artist, would it not be already there? The teacher had vehemently affirmed that of course it would, for it was there in all of us, but in the artist it could become a monster.

Lowering the cup, he said, "You look absolutely beautiful tonight. You always do, but tonight you do especially."

Savoring his words, she made no reply. It was odd how the pace of life seemed painfully slow at times and yet exhilaratingly fast at others. Only weeks before, she was outside this man. Now she was inside him. Then, she would have responded to his remark with suspicion. But as she looked into his eyes tonight she looked not for deception, for her heart, her mind, all of her, told her unequivocally that deception was not to be part of her concern.

Momentarily he asked, "What are you looking for?"

"In your eyes?"

"Yes, what are you looking for in my eyes?"

She smiled. "Not a thing, actually. I've already found it. And it's all that I want in all the whole wide world."

He watched until her lips had finished speaking the words, then after a deep breath he gave a little laugh and said, "You know, there is actually a lot of frost on the inside of this window. Maybe we should have accepted another table."

"Um, your phone is ringing, I think."

He retrieved the instrument and without looking for the ID, opened it and answered cheerily, "Hello."

"Well, hello there."

"Yes?"

"You don't know my voice?"

166

His eyes sought Martina's. "Uh, Gretchin?"

"That's right. Gretchin Wheeler, I would say *in the flesh,* but that might give you the idea that I'm in the nude."

"Hi, Gretchin," he returned, his eyes still upon Martina's. "What's up, as they say?"

"Who says that, for God's sake?" she demanded teasingly.

He cleared his throat. "Americans do, Americans say that. So, what is up?"

"Maybe my blood is up, Stanley. What's up with you?"

Raising his eyebrows for Martina's benefit, he said, "Gretchin, you sound like you are a little tipsy tonight, yes?"

"Wow, that's an old term," she retorted mischievously. "Where'd you learn that one, get it out of some Russian-English dictionary?"

"I do not know," he answered truthfully. "I suppose I heard it somewhere. Maybe it is British."

"Who cares, right? But no, I'm not drunk, just a little wild."

"Okay."

"But listen, my man, I've got a project in mind. See if you want to help me with it."

"What kind of project is this?"

"Actually, I want to do a series of nudes, self-portraits, actually. And I need someone to take some photographs for me to work from."

"And a mirror will not work for that project?"

"I hate working from a mirror. I need photos, big photos, color, lots of skin. You could come to my studio, or I could come to yours. Do you have a couch?"

"Uh, yes. Yes, I do. I have a couch."

"I'd pay you, of course, I mean, whatever's fair. I'm just a school teacher, a poor artist who has to teach. How much would you charge, Stanley, to photograph my nude body?"

He raised his eyebrows again. "Thank you for considering me, Gretchin, but I think I will not do it, I will pass, as they say."

"Ah, come on, where's the Russian man in you?"

"Actually, Gretchin," he answered, "the Russian man is very much there in me, and I hope it always will be there."

"That's the spirit."

"But no, I will pass. Listen, Martina and I are having dinner just at this time now, at a restaurant, and I am looking into her eyes just now across the table. It is very funny, yes?"

There was a pause, then, "Oh God, I'm sorry. Just forget the project, the whole idea, okay? I'm sorry, Stanley. Can I talk to her?"

"Yes, Gretchin?" said Martina, when she had taken the phone.

"Martina, I'm *really sorry*. I offered him a photography project, but I don't think it would have worked, so just tell him to skip it, okay? And I'm sorry again for bothering you two. Enjoy the rest of your dinner, okay? Sorry."

He took the phone again and closed it, his eyes on the platinum hair. Then he asked, "Do you want to know about her project?"

A smile. "Not really. You can tell me later, on the way home. But it won't be a surprise. I wouldn't put anything past her. And what exactly are you smiling at, Mr. Osipov? You seem very happy."

"I *am* happy," he replied, "I am happy that I have the rest of the whole evening just to look at you."

"Well, I hate to put a damper on your lust, sir, but we should get busy. We have to make plans, we have to decide about everything tonight. Time, I think, has run out."

On Saturday Martina awoke with a pleasant headache resulting more from physical fatigue than from the fear that seemed to be dogging her. She blinked repeatedly, cleared the sleep from her eyes with the sheet, and turned onto her side, pulling the covers up to her cheek. They had spent Friday together, and now she was actually tired from it, wonderfully tired. He had called early Friday to suggest they take the day off and go into the city. Maggie had patted her on the shoulder, turned her around, and given her a teasing push, promising to arrange a substitute for her class, and she had gone, responding to the sheer caprice of it. It had all been strange, mystical, as if like teenagers they were eloping with only Maggie to know. He had asked her to wear something comfortable, so she had worn jeans, sneakers, a cotton sweater, all of it giving her a sense again of the freedom she knew in her youth in coming to the West. It had been a glorious day, and now she could dream about it. Pulling the covers up, she closed her eyes.

"They won't let you take your camera through the museum," she warned.

"I will give it up."

Later, at the table in the museum's café, she asked, "Are you undressing me?"

"Yes," he confessed, "I am."

"And you without a camera."

After that, standing before a Monet, she felt his eyes again, undressing her. She did not turn to confront him, but closed her eyes and allowed him to continue. And then she heard his voice next to her ear.

"You are beautiful," he whispered.

Turning to him, "You seem very anxious for us to be together. Can you wait?"

Snuggling into the pillow under the blankets, she open her eyes and blinked again. His touch was gone, and love was not true. His arm was not around her, and love was not true. Love was a lie that nature told and spread ubiquitously. But if love was not true, *this* love was true. If men were not true, *this* man was true. All of it was true, for she believed it to be true, as true as life, as true as death. Arising, she took up her robe and went into the bathroom.

In the shower she gently rinsed shampoo and conditioner from her hair, then readjusted the water temperature. Before using the cinnamon soap they had bought together she put it to her nose to refresh her image of the little store. Then, under the streams, she worked the speckled bar into a soft fresh cloth and began to wash herself. The sweet lather she spread over her skin was intoxicating, even as he was intoxicating, though he was not there. *But he was there, and his hands were moving over her, his lips kissing her, his arms encircling her, his hands pulling her to himself.* In the hissing water she looked down to see the remnants of the cinnamoned suds disappear and wondered why life must be like that—beautifully here but quickly gone.

In the kitchen Maggie looked up from her magazine and said, "Richard called last night."

"What did he want? Is there any coffee left?"

"Well, I've been sitting here for an hour, but, yes. Sit down, I'll get it. Your hair looks nice, the new dryer?"

"Yes. I like it. It weighs nothing, I think."

"Try this, dear. Hazelnut."

"Um. I thought I smelled hazelnut. Very good, wonderful. So, what did Richard want?"

"He said he was just keeping up to date."

"What did you say?"

"I told him nothing, dear. He said he might call you today, on your cell."

"What did you have for breakfast?"

"Cereal, dear. Want some? Are you all right, dear?"

Submitting to eye contact, Martina replied softly, "Yes."

"Sure?"

Then, sarcastically, "Well, when I got out of bed this morning the mirror whispered a few strange things in my ear. It may have looked me in the face, but it whispered in my ear."

"About?"

"My age."

The green eyes were cool. "Mirrors will do that. And you took it well?"

"Not really."

The green eyes blinked. "I know the empty feeling that follows the reception of such communications. Once my mirror told me I could just stop worrying about who the fairest in the land was."

"Long list, Maggie?"

"Extensive."

Smiling, "I think we might have the same wizard fooling with our mirrors."

Maggie simply shrugged.

"God, I hate wizards."

"Now, now, dear. And how was yesterday?"

"Wonderful, it was *so* nice. Thanks for finding the substitute. Any problems with the class?"

"No problems, no. So, everything's the same with you and Stanley?"

"Yes."

"I suppose I didn't need to ask. You have that far-away look."

"Oh, yes? And how far is that, how far away am I looking, Maggie?"

A sigh. "I don't know, dear. Maybe, all the way to Moscow."

"Those green eyes of yours are perceptive, they always were."

But Maggie closed her eyes and looked away. Her mother had always told her just to shut her eyes at the bad parts in films so as not to dream about them later. When she grew up she discovered that the bad parts were not just in the movies. Life had presented so very many things for her to shut her eyes at. Now she opened them to watch as Martina poured cereal and milk and then began to eat.

"You know, dear," she said, "sometimes, I pretend to be blind, too."

"I find that hard to believe, Maggie, since you find it so annoying when I do it."

"Yes, but I only do it for moments, unbearable moments." Then picking up the magazine again, she queried, "Do you like the cereal? It's a new kind. Don't break a tooth on the nuts."

"No."

Turning a page, then another, Maggie wondered why everything had to seem so empty sometimes, like the pages of a magazine. It was all like that, all of it—the people you knew, the situations you lived through, the ideas you encountered—the whole pathetic parade seemed an endless stream of uninteresting images and meaningless words. You were expected to look, to read, to give your attention, your assent, your affection. You cared for none of it, but nevertheless, found yourself turning the pages of life, looking at the images, reading the words.

Finished, Martina sipped her coffee. "You're quiet," she said. "See anything in there?"

"It's a magazine, dear. There's nothing in a magazine."

"Oh, Maggie, what are we going to do without each other?"

"Yes, well, I have no idea what I'm going to do without you. You will have him, and I will have memories of you. I suppose, it's that simple." And at times, she thought, it did seem to be that simple, that dreary. The things you were supposed to want, seemed meaningless, lifeless. The things you wanted, you weren't supposed to have. The things you had were always eventually taken away from you, and you were left with no choice but to say goodbye to them and accept their loss. Often she recalled her dream when she was twelve, of a strange dog running away from her, of her calling after it. The next morning her mother told her that Tellie had died in his sleep during the night. The family had taken the great Setter in as a stray before Maggie was born. She had only known life with him there as watchdog, companion, friend, confidante, and yet now he had passed and was gone. Even as Maggie listened to the words that he was dead she could feel the grief beginning to overcome her mind. Each morning before school, Tellie had walked her to the gate and received the little piece of toast she gave him. In the evening, when she studied, he had lain at her feet, sometimes resting his head upon her shoe. And in his old age, nearly sightless, he had followed her from room to room throughout the house, unwilling to leave her for a moment. She had fed him, walked him, given him treats, and expected that he would always be there. Within a week of his passing, her grief became acute and she could not go to school, for she could not bear walking to the gate without him. But then, oddly, she dreamed of him. In the dream everything seemed to be fading away and Tellie had escaped through the gate and was running away, joyfully running away. When she called to him he stopped and turned and looked at her and with his eyes told her he had loved her. Then he turned away from her and ran, and she let him go.

The sudden ringing of Martina's phone gave them both a start. Quickly reading its screen, she rolled her eyes, took a moment to muster patience, and answered, "Yes. Hello, Richard. . . . Fine, thanks. . . . Yes. . . . Sure. . . . Well, give me twenty minutes or so. . . . Sure. . . . All right, see you then. . . . Bye." Then she closed the instrument and reached for her cup, which was empty.

Maggie only stared.

Martina gave an ominous groan, putting her cup back down. "I suppose I don't need more caffeine before seeing him. He's picking me up in a few minutes. He said he wants to talk, see how things are going."

Laying the magazine down, Maggie said defensively, "I didn't tell him anything, dear."

Martina gave the saucer and cup a deliberate push. "I know you didn't. That guy. I'm sorry, but there's just something about that bastard that makes me sick. I don't even want to get in the car with him, I find him so revolting. I don't want to go, but I guess I have to."

"We've both come to loathe him, haven't we?"

"God, is that the word? Why is it that some people make my stomach ache? Most people, I'm fine with. I meet new people every day, and I either like them or I don't, or a little of both, and everything's fine. But then, some people give me the dirty creeps, like they're vomiting on me. I don't know why, but it's that way for me with Richard."

"Maybe, you're sensing he has one or two screws loose."

"Thanks, I needed that, Maggie, and right before I get in the car with him."

"Sorry, dear. I'm sure you'll be all right, he probably just wants to talk and, you know, do the grimness thing. But you might want to go get dressed now."

"So, you're going to stick with me in this?"

"With your Russian guy, your *man*? I don't think you needed to ask that, dear."

"No," replied Martina apologetically. "No, I didn't."

CHAPTER 12

When the charcoal-gray sedan pulled up across the street, Martina, already wearing her coat, opened the door quickly and went out. She hurried, hoping he would not honk. He sat motionless, his face deadpan and his gaze fixed forward, like a robot. He had left the engine running, as if to say that she should not keep him waiting. She crossed the street, opened the passenger door, and got in.

"Hi, Richard," she offered, snapping the seatbelt into place.

"Good morning," he returned coldly. He did not look at her, but dropped the shift lever and slowly accelerated.

For a full minute he said nothing, but simply drove, staring through the windshield. He pretended to be concerned for the traffic, for pedestrians. Obviously he had no destination in mind, as he kept the sedan within the neighborhood. When he suddenly adjusted the rearview mirror and cleared his throat she looked over at him and then away.

"How is the situation with Mr. Osipov?" he queried distantly.

When two little girls, waiting to cross at a corner, waved to her she returned the wave and smiled. Both girls, grinning happily, held up candy for her to see. Then she took a deep breath and said, "Well, um, I guess I should tell you that Mr. Osipov and I have fallen in love, actually, and are planning to be married."

Following a soundless few seconds, he asked, "You mean, as part of the case?"

"No," she answered, quelling her shock. "No, I mean we have actually fallen in love with each other."

He made a clucking sound with his tongue before asking, "Have you had sex with him?"

The odor of his cologne made the compartment seem smallish. She replied frigidly, "That is not your business."

"Really? The whole thing is my business, every detail of it."

Declining to reply, she watched the street ahead, the passing cars.

"Did you hear what I said?" he asked impatiently. "Pay attention."

"Uh, yes," she answered. "Yes, I did."

It was bizarre, she thought, to be riding in his car as he drove them nowhere. His cold death hands gripping the steering wheel reminded her of what Father had told her in her youth, that there were people who lived as if inhabited by death, who only seemed to repel every truly living organism that came near.

"Well?" he demanded insistently. "What do you have to say for yourself?"

For some reason, she thought of the little girls who had waved and shown their candy. Drawing her breath slowly, she replied, "Richard, I revealed my identity. I told him who I was."

He held silent until he had turned a corner, then he asked, "How much did you tell him?"

"Only about me. I told him I was an advisor to the Agency. I didn't give him any details or names."

This time, his silence endured. He began to make his way back to the house. Still he would not look at her. When he had pulled up in front of the house he said, "I'll have to discuss this with my own people. I'll get back to you. Do the others know?"

"Only Maggie."

Keeping his foot on the brake, his hands on the steering wheel, he commanded unemotionally, "Don't discuss it with them. I'll tell them myself. It's in the Agency's hands now. Don't leave. Don't go anywhere."

When she sensed he had finished she pulled the door lever. She felt herself get out, close the door, and then walk up the pavement and climb the steps. Inserting and turning the house key seemed difficult, as if she was unable to accomplish something in a dream, but then she saw her hand push the door inward, and she stepped inside. Once, she looked toward the street, but the car was gone. Closing the door seemed easy, and she saw her hand turn the deadbolt. As she was hanging her coat in the middle closet she heard a voice and turned to see Maggie, her face drained, her green eyes large with fear. She felt herself smile at her. Then she heard Maggie's voice again. Maggie was speaking to her, and she was hearing her as she spoke.

"My Lord, you look strange, dear."

"What?"

"*Weird* is a better word. God, you look creepy. What did he say?"

"What?"

"Everything all right? You're a little incoherent, I think. What did he say?"

Then, as if the dreaming had ended, Martina smiled intentionally, consciously, and answered, "He didn't say much."

Patiently, "What did he say?"

"Well, I told him."

"All right. What then?"

"I need something to drink, strong tea or something." Closing the closet door and following Maggie into the kitchen, she said, "Don't worry. Worry is a useless exercise in pain."

"Yes, dear, we all know about worry, but what did he say? Look, just tell me a little more, okay?"

Pushing her hair back with her hands, Martina took a seat at the table. "I simply told him that Stanley and I loved each other and planned to be married. I also told him that I had revealed my identity."

The green eyes closed and then opened, crystalline and shining. "Oh. Oh my." And then, shaking her head slowly, she said, "Good luck, little girl, good luck to us all."

Martina closed the top drawer of her desk and looked up at the old clock. It was Wednesday afternoon, and she was alone in her classroom. She did not look at the clock for information, but for sympathy. A relic of the analog days, the timepiece had survived well beyond its rightful lifespan, despite the intentions of nearly everyone to replace it with a more accurate, digital instrument. Although it was she who had saved it, she saw it as a survivor. Not that she believed everything should be saved, of course, and perhaps most things should be let go, but she did feel that a few things—those which seemed necessary for connecting her to the past and refreshing her sense of the continuity of life—must be saved and cherished. Now, as she looked into the clock's wise old face she smiled, as if to a friend, and saw that her smile was being returned. She knew that lifeless material objects had a penchant for doing that. Having dismissed the class thirty minutes earlier, she looked around at the empty desks, her own desk, the blackboard, itself another relic she had saved. They all seemed friendly. Life had given her few friends, but surely these inanimate things were among them.

And she needed friends, for the people around her seemed to be rapidly falling away. Richard had begun to do his work. Bradley had been called and informed. Gretchin had been called. Richard had told them in his own laced words what had happened and that the Agency was considering the situation. Bradley's subsequent response to her was to ask why she hadn't been able to keep things professional. But it was his look that she recalled now, for it was one of purest contempt. To him she had become a member of the lowest species on earth, a traitor of her country. Gretchin called to ask why she had gone and screwed things up, maliciously emphasizing the word *screwed.*

Now, alone with her inanimate friends, she leaned back in the old chair and sighed under the weight of knowing she had betrayed the world she lived in. The face of the old clock did not actually smile upon her, but the hands that expressed its heart kept moving. Suddenly she stood up, collected her satchel and coat, and left. Her footsteps seemed clamorous in the empty hallway, and she was relieved to reach the open courtyard. In minutes she was driving along 5th Street at the edge of East Oak Lane, toward Olney, away from the world.

He was there, working in the kitchen. They were to make dinner together and then spend the rest of the evening packing things up. The past was fast catching up with them, but they must work in the present. The rest of it, the tomorrows to see, to live through, to enjoy, they would commit to hope.

She was glad to have him there as she worked in the kitchen. Never in her life had she been domestic, but that didn't matter now. They were there together, and she was simply doing whatever she thought she might be able to do to expedite things through the moment. He sat at the table and watched as she unwrapped, washed, and buttered the fish. She enjoyed having him watch her, but was relieved when he put music on.

"I know that piece," she said, "Wieniawski's *Legend*."

He beamed happily. "Yes, of course. I am so glad you know it. Oistrakh, world's greatest violinist. It is the whole album. There are many short pieces on it. I will just let it play."

Then, when she was cutting the bread, she felt his hands slip around her waist and his arms encircle her. She felt his lips on the back of her neck and closed her eyes in the sweetness of it. "The knife is sharp," she protested, "be careful." And when his arms loosened she put the knife down and turned to kiss him. When he stopped her, giving her a gentle kiss on the nose, she whispered, "None of that. I don't want any of that. Well, maybe a little of that, but more of this." And she kissed him deeply.

Then he released her and left the kitchen, but she knew he would come back. Life was like that too, she thought, sometimes it returned to you the things that were yours. When he was gone she played the game, pretending to be blind, doing everything carefully. Then he was there again, and she was overjoyed, for she was in her darkness and needed to feel him.

"Do not tell me," he laughed gently. "You are playing your game."

"Yes," she chuckled, keeping her back to him. "Yes, my game."

"But you will not care if I look at you, yes?"

Adjusting the heat under the pot of broccoli, she replied, "Not at all. What do you see?"

"I see blond hair, German hair, beautiful, blond German hair."

"Platinum, Mr. Osipov."

"I know this. It is not a correction," he protested.

"What else do you see?"

"A very thin neck."

"Yes?"

"And I see the rest of you, your shoulders, your back, your bottom, your legs. It is all very symmetrical."

"*Symmetrical*, is that the best you can do? But you are stimulated? You are a visually stimulated man."

"Well, you know, I am one of those photographer guys."

"Is that all you see, then?"

"That is all I see from back here."

"Shall I turn around?"

"No, no, do not do it. I will imagine the rest of you, for right now."

"Um."

When everything was ready they spread a fresh cloth upon the table and sat down to eat. They were quiet and ate slowly.

At length she said, "We should really hurry."

"Why?"

"We're eating like we want to slow the world down."

"So?"

"We have a lot to do."

"I know this," he admitted, his eyes on her hair, "but I want you to know that everything is wonderful, the fish, the broccoli, everything is wonderful, I like it. And you are even a good bread slicer."

She closed her eyes and whispered, chuckling, "Anytime."

But then he asked soberly, "We are not pretending, are we?"

"To be blind?"

He shook his head. "No, I mean, about life. We are not pretending about life, yes?"

"No," she answered, "we are not pretending. That would be a very stupid thing to do. So, if you see me doing it, please stop me, okay?"

"I am sorry," he said then, looking down at his plate. "I am sorry that I have brought all of this to your life."

She shook her head and replied sternly, "Don't say that, Stanley."

"I would say that I am sorry I love you," he continued, "but I cannot say that. I think that your life was a perfectly straight line, but I have warped it."

She did not reply, but for some reason, pictured him again as she had seen him at the beginning, his face as he stood in the next aisle. She imagined she was speaking to him again and then leaving her aisle and coming into his, walking toward him, searching his face.

Then she said, "I'm sorry, too."

"Yes?"

"I'm sorry that I'm not twenty."

He merely smiled at this, but then said, "That is very funny, as they say."

She did not reply.

Then he said, "What you are is what you are, and that is all I want. I do not want you at twenty, I want you just as you are now."

"And I want you," she replied, "just as you are."

CHAPTER 13

Retreating to observe an application of gesso to water-stretched paper, Gretchin frowned, unhappy with herself. "Piling it on again, huh? Stupid," she muttered. But she would forgive herself, since it was Friday and she had had a bad week. Earlier that day a student had actually eaten paint in front of her, which was odd in her quiet suburban middle school. And what had not gone wrong that week? But now she was home, in her studio, and she could shake it all off. Later, she would walk down to the Ritz and see a film, something very nice and sexy.

Grabbing a towel as the phone rang, she wiped her hands and looked down at the screen. With a shake of her head, she pressed Speaker, and took a seat. Normally she disliked technology, but when it allowed her to distance herself from something or someone unpleasant she loved it.

"Hi, Richard," she said, still wiping her hands.

"Yes, Gretchin," he returned, his voice icy. "I'm calling to let you know the latest."

"Yes?"

"We're dismissing the team, *all* of you."

And there he let it stand, as if assured that the statement would, like a blade, run through to her heart. She sensed not only his weird satisfaction that he was hurting her, but his utter faith in power. She wondered whether she had ever, in all her life, found anyone to be so loathsome.

"Wow," she retorted facetiously. "That's cute."

"This is serious, Gretchin," he warned.

"Oh, yeah?"

His voice became menacing. "What do you think, that it's *not*?"

"Oh, I'm sure it is, Richard, I'm sure it is. But listen, tell me something."

"What?"

"You're getting your jollies, aren't you?"

Filling his voice with disgust, he retorted, "Stupid question."

"Actually," she returned, "that was not my question, it was a setup for my question."

"Which is what?"

"These jollies of yours, are they personal or corporate?"

"Another stupid question," he pronounced unemotionally. "Listen, your relationship with the Agency is dissolved. Forget your association with us. Never refer to it. Do you understand?"

"Oh, sure."

"Do you *really* understand?"

"Sure."

"I'll talk to the others. Then you're free to talk to them."

"So," she said, "you just dictate what people can remember or not remember and who they can talk to, and when, and all that. I mean, just *dictate* it. Wow, that's impressive. God must really have to consider his options around people like you."

Ignoring her, he said, "I won't be talking to you again. Your relationship with us is ended."

"Well, now that's too bad," she added quickly, for she sensed he was about to hang up. "I was going to get Stanley to photograph the tattoo on my fucking ass and send it to Putin."

"Goodbye, Ms. Wheeler."

"Take a walk, prick." And when she had pressed the Off button, she uttered, "Prick. Goddamn federal prick."

In his office Bradley closed his briefcase and locked it. But instead of reaching for his coat, he sank deeper into his leather chair and put his head back. He loved his office. He had decorated it himself, so that nearly everything in it reminded him of something in his life. On his wall, just above his degree, framed in wood, he had hung his war photo of his father, framed in gold. Beside these he had pinned to the cork panel his American flag stretched out.

He jumped when the phone buzzed and then quickly grabbed the handset without checking the display. "Hello," he said, slumping in the chair, "Mr. Hopkins here."

"It's Richard."

"Yes, hello, Richard. How are things going—I mean, with Martina and everything?"

"Well, you tell me. I'm calling to let you know that we're dismissing the team. We're dismissing all of you. Your relationship with the Agency is dissolved as of now."

Catching his breath and staring at nothing, Bradley felt himself suddenly falling away. For a moment, he simply could not speak. Then, incredulous, he asked, "Why?"

"*Why?* You can't be serious, that's a ridiculous question."

"But—"

"Forget your association with us. Never refer to it. Do you understand?"

"But, why *all* of us?"

"That was the decision. Live with it."

He sat forward. "But you know who the culprit is."

"*Do* I, Mr. Hopkins?"

He hesitated, moistening his lips. "Yes. It's Martina. You know that. I mean, that's what this is all about."

"*Is* it? Is that what it's all about? *You* are telling *me* what it's all about? You're telling *us*, the Agency, what it's all about? What it's about, very simply, is that you, all of you, are dismissed, permanently. And you are not to talk to the others. I've just called Gretchin and will go to see Martina. Wait until Monday—yes, at least Monday—before you talk to them—don't even think about it. Do you understand me?"

"Yes," he murmured feebly.

"This is official. Just keep your distance until it's wrapped up."

"But, it's not fair."

"What? What is that word you just used?"

Shifting the handset to his other ear, he replied, "I said, it's not fair. I like this work. I enjoy serving the Agency, helping my country. I didn't do anything wrong. I'm innocent and I don't like being punished for what someone else has done. I've acted responsibly, that's all. I have acted responsibly and honorably. This team has completed many assignments, and we haven't failed, and now, because of one *woman,* you want to punish all of us. That's not fair."

And now viciously, "Listen. You don't tell me what's fair, *I* tell *you*, okay?"

"Well," he stammered, his voice rising to a shout, "well, I'm telling *you* right back. It was Martina. I didn't do anything wrong, not a thing." Then he added, "And I never did like her, either. I always did think there was something wrong with her."

"Is that right? And why didn't you share that with us? You see there, that's exactly how you're all connected."

"It was one person, one *woman.* I didn't do anything. Nobody did anything, except Martina."

"Well, this way, we know we've got you all."

"Why can't I have another team? Why can't I have another chance, another team?"

"There will be no other team for any of you."

Shaking his head, as if he could be seen, he said again, "It's not fair, *Richard.*"

"Goodbye, Mr. Hopkins."

The line went dead, and he was left staring at the door, as if Richard, the Agency, the rest of the team, had in a single moment all abandoned him. Yes, they had gone through that door and taken with them his service to his country. And what had he done to deserve it? He had been nothing less than conscientious in blessing his country and cursing the Russians. He had served faithfully and had been rewarded with suspicion and punishment. Still incredulous, he stared at the door.

Rolling his chair back, he pulled on his coat, lifted the briefcase, and walked out. He did not take a last look, as he usually did upon leaving for the day, at the photo of his father. Neither did he lock the door, for although he prided himself in never failing to secure his office, he had other thoughts in mind as he left the building.

The yellow Corvette, like a lone icon, rested in the nearest space on the empty lot. He had declined the school board's offer of a dedicated parking space, for he expected to be the first one to arrive in the morning, the last to leave at night, making the special favor unnecessary. Indeed, this diligence and sense of honor he had applied to every facet of his career, for all to see and to credit. Now as he approached the car it unlocked itself. He got in and sank into the soft leather seat that had warmed itself for him.

Inserting the key, he started the engine. The interior of his car was a beautiful world, one he had created for himself, one in which the principle of cause and effect had its rightful place. His car was a microcosm of his larger life. For his diligence and faithfulness he had been duly rewarded by everyone in every area of his life, every area, that is, except this one, the team. He could understand Richard's coldness toward him, for he was simply an agent of an agency, one not known for its warmth. As for Martina and Maggie, he had known the first day he arrived as principal that they disliked him. People rarely disliked him—why did they? And why were they so together in their disdain? As for Gretchin, well, her dislike for him was to be understood for what it was, the typical lunacy of a wacky female artist. Yes, his service with the team was a failure. But he would take action, he would do something. Then he opened his phone and placed the call.

"Martina," he said jovially, "this is Brad."

"Yes, Bradley," she replied. "What do you want?"

"Richard called me," he said coldly.

"Yes?"

"I'm not supposed to talk to you."

"He called about that?"

"Well, not exactly. He called about your *affair*, your affair with Stanley Osipov, our Russian infiltrator." Then, as if he had successfully punched her in the mouth, he let himself settle lower into the Corvette's luxurious leather and waited for her response.

Momentarily she said, "I don't like your tone, Bradley."

"Well, guess what? He's dismissing the entire team, all of us. That's the way he said it. He doesn't trust any of us, how do you like that?"

"Yes."

"What do you mean by *yes*?" he demanded angrily. "What kind of response is that?"

"Well, I'm sorry, Bradley."

"That's not good enough, Martina. It was your fault, and I told him that. It was all your fault. Nobody else did anything wrong, just you and this Russian—you know, the man you were supposed to be extracting information from. So, don't just say you're sorry, because that's not good enough."

"If that's what Richard said, that's what he said, Bradley. That's the Agency. I'm sorry."

"Well, I want back in. I want another chance, because nobody did anything wrong, except you. And guess what, I want you to do something about this."

"I'm sorry."

"I want back in," he blubbered, nearly frantic. "You are the culprit here, what you've done is heinous, and you have been caught. I haven't done anything wrong. I'm innocent here, and I don't want to be blamed at all. You did it, I didn't. I want back in."

"What am I supposed to do about it?"

"I don't know and I don't care. Just see him, or something. Tell him I had nothing to do with your affair. And make him believe it."

"Actually, he'll be here soon. He called, he's coming by. But my guess is that there's nothing I can do about the Agency's decision. Richard hasn't told me himself, actually. This is the first I've heard. And he told you not to talk to me?"

"Yes."

"Then, why are you?"

"Listen, I didn't know a thing about your affair. Tell him that. Tell him that you acted completely on your own and that I'm innocent, that I acted in good faith and have always acted in good faith. You were the team leader, and you can at least vouch for my honor, tell him, tell the Agency, that I always discharged my duty honorably. I want him to assign me to another team. That's all I want."

"I'll have to talk to him. He hasn't told me anything. But I seriously doubt I can do anything about the Agency's decision, whatever it was."

"You're the one having the affair, Martina, not me. Why should I suffer, or Gretchin or Maggie?"

"It's not an affair, Bradley. We love each other."

In nearly but not quite a whisper he replied, "Horseshit."

"Bradley, I think there's nothing I can do. I've already told Richard no one else was involved. I think he just wants to make sure. I'm sorry, Bradley. There's nothing I can do."

He waited for just a moment and then queried maliciously, "What about your retirement?"

"My pension?"

"Yes," he hissed.

"What about it, Bradley?"

"You're going to need it, aren't you, unless you've hit the old ladies' lottery?"

"Yes, I will need it. *We* will need it."

"What if I fix it so you don't get it, not a wretched lira of it?"

"And just how would you do that?"

"I'm the principal here, stupid. I know everybody in the school system. I know the people and I know the tricks. I know who sleeps with

195

whom, and I know the maneuvers they go through to get what they want. And I've thought of a few pranks of my own, lady. Trust me, I can do it."

He felt victorious. No one had to tell him he had won. He put his head back against the seat. He did not attempt to interrupt the silence on the line, but simply savored the moment and waited for the response. And then he heard her voice.

"I have one thing to say to you, Bradley. Listen carefully. I worked through all my career for that pension, and I expect to receive it. When I should have retired I stayed on because you asked me to. I earned that pension. It is mine, *ours.* Now listen very, very carefully. My guess is that no one else is listening to us right now, but even if they are, this is what I have to say to you. Stanislav Osipov worked for the old KGB all over Europe throughout the Cold War. He knows people, trust me. And those people are more dangerous than anything you can imagine, they are far more dangerous to you than the people on your school board are to us. You had the same training for the team as I did. The KGB was considered the most effective intelligence agency in the world. And if you think the KGB is defunct, you're fantasizing. What do you think, they all just quit and sat around drinking vodka and reading *The New York Times*? They may have a different name now, but they're still there, and they will be there tomorrow and the day after that. You have no idea what those people will do to you, if you even touch what belongs to Stanislav Osipov. Now, you're already on the wrong side of the CIA. If you think that's *noir*, try falling afoul of the KGB friends of this man. God!

You would go to hell in a lot of pain, mister. So, do you understand me, *Brad?* Are we on the same page?"

What followed was a long silence, one long enough, in fact, for her to watch Maggie let Richard in at the front door, usher him to a seat on the couch, and hang his coat in the middle closet. Then she heard Bradley's response.

"Yes, all right, okay, yes, I understand, Martina. Forget it. Don't worry. I'm sorry, I'm not going to do anything. Don't worry."

Her tone was matter-of-fact. "I won't. Goodbye."

Closing the phone, she went to the front room. "Good afternoon, Richard," she offered as she gave Maggie a roll of the eyes and then sat to face him.

"Yes, hi," he responded coldly.

Maggie put in, "I'll just make some tea. Richard, can I bring you some cake, would you like some cake?"

"No," he blurted, shaking his head. "And no tea, either, just no, I'm fine."

Accepting this, she asked, "Martina?"

Placing one hand upon the other on her lap, Martina replied in an obviously courteous tone, "Well, yes, thank you, Maggie, that would be very nice."

"Is English breakfast all right?"

"Yes, wonderful, thanks."

"Dark?"

Watching as he shifted impatiently at this, Martina answered, "Yes, thank you, Maggie, that would be good."

Then Maggie turned to him again and asked in her most polite tone, "Sure?"

Incredulous, he stared at her. "Yes, I'm sure."

"Sure," she replied pleasantly. "Just checking."

He blinked at her, as if waiting for her to leave, and when she had gone he cleared his throat, then said, "The Agency, Martina, has come to a decision as to what to do with you."

For some reason, she felt a calm come over her at his words. She had worried that she might be nervous, but now was inexplicably steady. Savoring the serenity, she did not respond, but simply presented him with a tranquil smile.

If the offer of tea and cake had annoyed him, the smile he now encountered reached his core. Spitefully he continued, "We have decided to dismiss the team."

"And what," she inquired pleasantly, "does that entail exactly?"

"It simply means our relationship with all of you is terminated—*period.*"

"What else?"

"Well," he replied coolly, his eyes dropping to her legs, "we could prosecute you, but we've decided not to."

"Why?" she asked, crossing her legs.

He frowned, but then put on a smile, as if to savor the opportunity she had given him to place his shot.

"Actually," he replied, pausing, apparently to enjoy the delivery, "because you are simply not worth the expense, that's why."

She nodded her acceptance, but said nothing.

Looking beyond her, he demanded, "What are the suitcases for?"

For just a millisecond she watched as he filled himself with anger, then she answered, "They're for traveling. Yes, and my coat is there, also."

He glared fiercely at her. "I thought I told you not to leave."

She did not reply, but continued to look at him placidly.

Placing the tip of his forefinger under his chin, he asked, "Where are you going? You know, you've betrayed your country, and so has he."

"*Betrayal* is a strong word," she returned.

He put his hands together. "You are both traitors."

"We simply fell in love and withdrew from our programs."

"Don't say *simply*, that's wrong. Don't say *simply*. You told each other about your programs."

"Yes, we did. Not in detail, but yes, we did. We fell in love, and—"

"Don't say that!" he raged. "Don't tell me that. Human attraction is no excuse for breaking your oath to secrecy. *Fell in love.* Ridiculous. You're an old woman, for God's sake, face it." He finished by taking a long deep breath to exhibit the fact that he was subduing his anger.

"So," she responded thoughtfully, "you see us as traitors, but you're not going to prosecute us."

"That's right, that's right, you have it, that's correct, um-hm. Congratulations, you have it. The Agency isn't going to prosecute, because you're not worth the expense. You know, Martina, you really did think too much of yourself. You were a mere advisor. I personally thought you were egotistical, that's right, and I thought you knew way too much about the operations of the program, to suit your ability, anyway. I'm sorry, but I have to be frank, you thought way too much of yourself, Martina. You were just an advisor, and you couldn't even handle that. And here we are, and I've been proven right. I mean, *fell in love,* what is that? We're talking about your oath, your honor, your country, and you betrayed it all for what? A Russian infiltrator, the enemy, for God's sake. I mean, admit it, it's disgusting. It's filthy, dirty, loathsome, and disgusting." He paused, glaring at her, as if expecting a response. Realizing she was not going to provide one, he asked, "So, now that you've done all this to yourself and to others, to all of us really, to everyone, to *me,* where will you go? What country would want you? This one doesn't want you anymore. What country is going to want you?"

Coolly she asked, "And we need one of those, right?"

"I don't know what your needs are," he replied with contempt, throwing her a wave of his hand, "and I don't care. But you have to live somewhere, don't be naive."

"Well, then, how about Russia?"

"Oh, oh," he chortled, "Russia. I don't think so."

"Well, actually," she said, "we may just stay here. We're not sure yet. We'll see."

"You're not sure, and yet you've packed your suitcases and your coat is ready," he mocked contemptuously. "Anyway, I've let the others know. You are—all of you—finished."

"I don't believe Maggie's heard from you. Have you, Maggie?"

Her green eyes twinkling, Maggie placed her laden tea tray upon the coffee table. "No, actually, I haven't, Martina," she replied sweetly. "I haven't heard a thing from you, have I, Richard? Now, here's some tea and something to refresh you, Richard, for your trip, just help yourself."

He did not look at her, but stood abruptly and offered, "Well, Martina can fill you in."

"I pretty much heard everything from the kitchen, Richard, that's okay."

He gave her a weary glance. "Look, can I just have my coat?"

Martina got up instantly. "Certainly," she replied. "Let me get it." When she had returned she handed it to him and then sat again, lifted the pot, and pour herself a cup of tea. She was aware that her hand was still steady.

"Is it dark enough, dear?" queried Maggie.

"It is, yes, thank you, Maggie. But then, you like it dark, too, don't you? Everything looks quite yummy."

"Thank you, dear."

After giving the coat a shake, he pulled it on, buttoned it, then peered down at Martina. Following a quick sniff, he asked, "So, does your *man* think the Russian program will succeed?"

She did not answer, but sipped the tea.

Then he said dismissively, "Goodbye."

Maggie followed him to the door. "Goodbye to you, now, Richard," she said cordially, holding it open for him.

But then he turned and looked at Martina as she sat in her chair with her tea. With utter disdain, he said to her, "If you were young, Martina, I'd be glad to wish that all your babies would puke on your shoulder and shit on your lap. But I can see there's no need for that."

Martina, not acknowledging him, simply sipped her tea.

But as he stepped out Maggie said to him, "But we *are* young, Richard, can't you see it?" Then she closed the door securely, as if to close him out forever. When she had taken a seat on the couch she rolled her eyes and said, "Whew, that's one corpse I'd never ask Jesus to raise. And now, I think I'll have a piece of cake." Then she looked across at the gray eyes and said, "What, no tears?"

"No, Maggie. No tears."

It was dark when the Voyager pushed its way northward through the cold of upper New York state. They had stopped to eat at dusk and were now armed with coffee and donuts against the next leg of the journey. The surrounding countryside, invisible to them now, seemed ominous and threatening, and the lonesome highway seemed to be leading them into oblivion. When she asked if it was as bleak as Siberia he answered simply that it was not.

"It's amazing how good these things are when you're traveling," she said after biting into a coconut-covered donut, "and of course, with fresh hot coffee, you never count the calories, you just lie down and die."

"You are too skinny to worry about it," he replied.

During the quieter moments, she could not help but think of Maggie. "I am worried about her," she said.

"Yes, I knew you were, I could tell. What does she plan to do now?"

"She wants to retire at the end of the school year and find a warmer climate. She loves Bermuda, or maybe she'll go to Italy. Poor Maggie."

"Teachers are not poor in America," he returned, "only in Russia." When she was quiet he said, "I am sorry. I made a joke, but I am sorry. You are feeling the guilt, yes?"

"I've made a vagabond of her, I think."

He shrugged. "We will go to visit her, or she will come to our home."

"And where will that be?"

At length he replied, "This is the home, and your sister's farm will be the home, and wherever we will be going after that. I am sorry, but the home is this car, yes, and wherever we will be going. We will try to see Maggie again. I do not know any other answer. I am sorry about it."

"There is nothing to be sorry about," she replied disinterestedly.

"You are hurt, and I am sorry. And Maggie is hurt. But I was not trying to fall in love, either." He shrugged again. "If we have the love for the woman, the friend is hurt. If we do not have the love for the woman, the woman is hurt. Nature makes it all work that way—we must make the choice, and then someone is hurt."

Then she asked, "Do you think, they will do anything, or just let us go like this?"

"Your people will do what they want to do, just like the Russians. They will probably let us go, I think, but there is an old joke, *You can leave if you can make it to the door.* And I keep thinking of the joke."

"So, what's your gut feeling, that they will try something?"

"I love this idiom *gut feeling*, I have heard it before. It is so much Russian. I have not used it, but I will try."

She looked at his dark form as he drove. "Maybe we should stay on task here. I'm talking about whether they're going to kill us or not. This is serious."

"Of course," he replied defensively. "I know this. I am totally believing you. But no one knows the answer to your question. Who knows this? Either they will kill us or they will not kill us. How can anyone know this until it happens?"

"Yes," she said, sighing, "like falling in love."

His eyes did not leave the highway. "You are not very happy tonight, I think."

She looked through her window, but could see nothing. All seemed dismally lonesome. "It seems so much like Germany out there," she said. "Do you think you will like Vermont?"

"Of course. It will be like Russia."

"But not like Siberia, you said?"

He shook his head. "That is very harsh. You would not want to live in Siberia in."

"You seem very certain of that."

"People do not live in Siberia, they exist there. And I do not think you are a person who only wants to exist. You want to live."

In the darkness his hands seemed strong as they manipulated the steering wheel, and he seemed strong as he piloted them through the night. She needed him to be strong, not to take care of her or to compete with her, but to take his place with her and to take his part with her.

CHAPTER 14

Bellagio, Italy, Summer 2008

Reaching behind her head to adjust the towel-covered pillow, Martina moistened her lips, closed her eyes, and made herself more comfortable. She had pulled one of the hotel lounge chairs to a shady spot to avoid being victimized by the sun. For nearly half an hour she had been trying to recall details of the vacation following the war. Surely they had stayed somewhere nearby. The car Father had brought them in was gray, the boat they had taken out was white. She had laughed and run as much as she wanted. She had eaten pasta. But that was all, no details to make it alive now. So often it seemed that her memory slept when she wanted it to be awake, only then to awaken when she wanted it to sleep. She loved memories, just as she loved to pretend, but she knew they were all the same, facts so altered by the mind that they were only useful as entertainment. Adjusting the pillow further, she wondered why the mind was like that, why it needed to redefine reality so that it was acceptable. And then a hand touched her bare foot, and she opened her eyes.

"I know you," she said. "I've seen you around here. You shine shoes, don't you?"

The man made no reply, but simply seated himself at the foot of her lounge chair, pushed the brim up on his very Italian-looking straw hat, and dropped a pair of women's shoes for her to inspect.

She continued, "And you do good work too. I have heard you're a rascal at times, but I think you're a hell of a shoe shiner."

"How much am I worth, would you say?" he asked, tweaking a toe of her stretched-out foot. "Do not cheat, now, beware."

"At least five lira, I'd say. Why, I've got it right here." She pretended to reach for a purse.

"Do not do it," he warned. "I want more."

"What do you want?"

"I want the woman, not the money." And he kissed the toe he had tweaked.

Raising her leg and touching his shoulder with her foot, she said, "You can have the woman. But not here, for both of you would be arrested and thrown into prison. And Italian prisons are more notorious than they are famous. You will have to wait until a more appropriate place presents itself. Then, yes, you may have her."

Pushing the hat brim up a little more, he turned his back to her, looked out across the water of Lake Como, and asked, "So, you still don't recognize anything?"

"No," she replied, frowning. "Somehow the atmosphere seems the same, but that's about it. I guess the water, something about the lake itself, seems familiar, too."

"Yes? Well, it is probably a lot dirtier now. It could have the same light, though, from the water, air, sun, and color, I think. I am pretty sure."

"There must be innumerable factors," she mused dreamily, "that cause Italian sunlight to look the way it does."

"Yes, yes, sure. Just the land and water reflections must be unique. But do you remember enjoying it?"

"Yes. It was sublime, even by the standards of a child's aesthetic. We loved it, we loved it." She laughed, recalling the joy itself, how all the family had all shared in it. And they had taken the joy back to Germany and shared it at home, talking among themselves of the *Italian splendor*. But then, had it been joy or something else? In fact, she was no longer certain what it had been or that it had been there at all. And she wondered again why the mind needed to do such things with reality. Suddenly she felt his hand on her foot again, and she said, "I wonder whether I will remember the way you kissed me the first time."

"Yes? You are wondering that? Do not worry about it, I will keep doing it to remind you."

"The way you did in Moscow, in front of your mother?"

He shrugged, still with his back to her. "We were married, so what could it matter? I was proud of you."

And then she laughed again. She was happy and had been so since they were married in Vermont. From the moment they stepped out into the light that day, she knew she could say he was truly hers and she was truly his. The melancholy of the past had gone and, she was certain, would never return.

"I like to hear you laugh," he said, not turning around.

With both hands she pushed her hair back, fixing her gaze upon him. She knew from his voice that he would soon be dreaming of the pictures he might take during the rest of their trip. The D3, slung diagonally, rested at the middle of his back. The short-zoom lens he was so proud of pointed directly at her, but its little cover made it blind. Sensuously she recalled the days just after the wedding, when its cover was off and it was able to see her. Of the thousands of pictures he took of her during those first days, at least half were nudes. After spending countless hours editing, printing, framing their favorites, they hung them on nearly every wall in the house. When Sophie visited she joked and said the place had been transformed into a Parisian art gallery that needed censoring. Recalling the sensuousness of it now, she curled her toes luxuriously and then nudged him with her foot.

"You are thinking," she said, her eyes closed. "What are you thinking? Or maybe you're dreaming of photographing all the Italian women out there?"

"That would not be bad," he admitted, looking into the distance. "And nude, of course."

"Of course."

"But I am thinking of the lake, the towns, the streets, the effects of the light of this place. I do not think a photographer could wish to have more than this, except, maybe, for the German model, such as you are."

"Venice is nice, too."

"I have been there," he said. "The dirty water of the canals is splendid."

"People don't use that word much anymore."

Ignoring this, he continued, "The whole city has the atmosphere of falling down. It is like a beautiful woman who is growing old."

She eyed him suspiciously. "An oblique reference to me, to my age, perhaps?"

"Of course."

"I take it that your reference wasn't negative, though?"

"It was sensually positive, how is that?"

"Practically literary. I'm impressed." But then, pointing a finger, she said, "I have wondered why you take so many pictures of my bottom."

"Nude bottom," he corrected, with a shrug. "The skin is soft and white, very photogenic, what can I say?"

"So, these photographs are flattering, in your opinion?"

"Certainly."

"And you are not saying my bottom looks younger than my face?"

Turning to face her, he replied, "Absolutely not. Your ass is as old as your face. You are so paranoid. You do not need to be paranoid, you have the skin of a baby."

Pleased, she gave him a shove with her foot and said, "Russian fool."

Then he looked away again, far away, and said he wanted to go and walk in the town. Slipping her feet into the shoes he had brought, and declaring the Italian sun to be potent even in the shade, she took his hand, and when she was standing, pulled him close and kissed him.

In their room at the hotel, which they had taken for the entire month of July, she bathed her face with water and blotted it with the fresh towel. She did not look long at herself in the little mirror above the ceramic bowl, for mirrors told you things you were not always ready to hear. As the weather had been hot since they had arrived in Italy, they found themselves making frequent returns to their room to rinse the perspiration from their faces, and sometimes, to make love.

She emerged from the tiny bathroom as he was fitting into place a longer zoom.

"Ready, then?" she asked.

"Of course. Russians are always ready."

"I meant, ready to go." Then she added, "And watch your behavior around Maggie, if you don't mind."

"Yes, I will. I am sorry."

"Goofball," she chortled, closing her purse with exaggerated effort. She called him this when he frustrated her in fun, which he loved to do. Although he had not yet brought her to genuine anger, she knew that in time he would and that she might be brought to cast at him a vitriol of evil. But for now, he seemed simply to need to harass her occasionally in his humor. Delighted, she bantered with him. The truth was, she loved to tease him. Whenever she found him brooding or to have been too long at his work, she tried bringing him back by saying something funny or doing something quirky. If nothing else worked, she clowned out a strip tease. Although his humor tended to be darker than hers, levity was a sphere in which they could pretend together and, in a sense, be blind together, blind to the sadness of the world around them.

Slinging the camera diagonally and pushing it around to his back, he asked in mock protest, "Just why do you keep calling me the *Goofball*? I am a sensitive Russian and I feel that I am being mislabeled."

She looked at him with suspicion. "A sensitive Russian? Really?"

He shrugged. "Well, I am a photographer, then. I am an artist."

"I'm moved."

"Yes, I am an artist, and you are a vicious school teacher, frustrated from years of not being allowed to deal with bad students. Now you are taking it out on me—a defenseless immigrant photographer."

As if he had been saying nothing, she asked, looking around her, "Where did I put my hat?"

"The big one?"

"Yes. No more sun, please. Where is it?"

"Probably on the bed," he returned innocently, "where we make love."

She looked askance at him. "Please. Moron."

"A new label," he muttered to himself.

"Out. We have to go, and I want some lunch."

"Why? You never eat very much. You buy the food, but you do not eat it."

Outside, she repositioned the hat. He had bought it for her before boarding the train in Milan. It was of a fine straw and had a black silk ribbon.

"It is perfect," he observed as she nudged the brim. "It is charming."

"Thank you, my husband bought it for me. He is a photographer and has very good taste."

As they began to walk he slipped his arm around her waist.

And then she said seriously, "I cannot wait to see her, Stanley."

"I know this," he replied and put his nose just above her shoulder to smell the fragrance of her skin. "What do you wish for?"

"For something to eat, maybe a salad."

"Ah," he complained. "You are so unromantic."

"Hungry."

"But you are so skinny."

"And maybe some wine. That would be nice."

As the shuttle boat eased away from the boarding platform next morning, on its way to Varenna, Martina took pictures with her tiny camera, first of the platform, then of Bellagio itself. When they were farther out she turned the camera off and dropped it back into her purse.

Standing behind her, Stanley, using a short zoom, moved closer to the railing to pull her profile into the viewfinder. When she was perfect he pressed the shutter release, moved slightly to the right, and pressed it again. He loved catching her in profile, although he preferred her without a hat.

Then they took a seat on a bench, away from the railing, and watched the water of the lake as the craft pushed it away. Nearby, people chatted and moved about, and some simply sat in silence and watched the water.

"Why do you think it is," he asked her, "that people always like to look at water?"

"Because it's powerful and free, I suppose."

He nodded but did not reply.

"You know," she said at length, "there are other women here, beautiful women, and you're not taking pictures of them, Mr. Osipov. Why is that?"

His voice low, he replied, "Yes, this is right, no pictures. It is because I do not want to get myself shot by the jealous husband or boyfriend, or even by my own wife."

Chuckling at this, she squeezed his hand and took in the air of the open lake. Then she took her hat off, placed it on her lap, and waited. If occasionally she found his fascination for her hair to be annoying, usually she found it to be flattering and ultimately comforting. She was not a voluptuous woman, she knew, and although men had always looked at her, she knew she could never compete with genuinely curvy women. Whatever else nature had given her, it was not voluptuousness. Her mystique was what it was, and it could be and should be no more than that. She did not consider competition with other women for the eyes of her husband to be a viable pursuit. From the very first, he had looked at her, and that was enough. Of all the objects of desire the sunlight and the shadows had presented to this image-conscious, image-driven man, she was the one that fascinated him the most. If there was a God, as Stanley had insisted there was, how could she ask him for more than this? It wasn't as if this man of hers ignored the physical beauty of other women. She had never expected that of him, for he was, after all, a photographer, an artist, an image-oriented male. She had seen him look at Gretchin's cleavage and at Maggie's eyes and skin. But she had also seen him look past them and all other women to rest his eyes, as if in finality, upon herself. And that was enough, that was really quite enough.

"Can I get you something to drink?" he asked.

She shook her head. "No thanks. Maybe I'll get something in Varenna. That would be nice, but—" and glancing around her, "it's a little close here."

Then she watched as he stood to take distance shots of the scenery, candids of individuals in the crowd, then more distance shots. She had seen him work like this before and had sarcastically accused him of being a paparazzo. But he had seemed hurt, and she had apologized. Only in candids, he had said, could he get the magic of the unaware soul.

She waited until he had replaced the lens cover, then whispered mischievously, "The woman in the polka dots was posing, I saw her, and besides, the man with her is Sicilian, I think."

He looked toward the couple, then asked, "Why do you think that he is Sicilian?"

"His clothes, anyone can see that. And I saw the way he looked at you."

He shot them a sober glance. "It is true?"

"No," she replied, "I was just kidding. I was jealous."

"You are being crazy."

She lowered her voice. "Kiss my ass."

"Do not be crude," he returned in mock protest. "You are not a Cossack, you are a school teacher, you are respected. Besides this, you know that I love kissing your, um, bottom."

Drawing her breath slowly, as if savoring his words, she looked out across the water. "It is certainly a splendid day, to use your word. Look at that glorious water."

"It is polluted, I think."

"Most beautiful things are." And then she said, "I cannot wait to see her. She will love turning her green eyes upon this part of Italy. Actually, there is an emerald color here that reminds me of her eyes."

"I have seen it. Yes, especially in the water. But, is this part of Italy warm enough for her?"

"It is, in the summer."

"So, when can I kiss your ass?"

Dreamily she replied, her eyes upon the distant haze. "Be quiet, I am occupied with beauty, not lust."

"Tell me what you see."

She shrugged. "It's hazy, the sunlight is blending everything into blue and gray and yellow."

"It is because of the humidity, I think." And then he said, "Your eyes are gray."

"You've told me that a hundred times. I know what color my eyes are."

"You remind me of a wolf."

"You see me as predatory?"

"Yes, of course. You came after me in the movie store, yes?"

"Not romantically."

"No, you were the predator spy, you were CIA, and I was only a poor Russian immigrant."

"What a liar," she chortled. "Immigrant? You were not an immigrant. You're the one who was the spy. Don't play innocent with me, *Vladimir*."

"This remark is politically incorrect," he protested. "The CIA are animals, they are wolves."

She shook her head. "It was you who came after me, in the restaurant, if I may bring it to your attention, sir."

"But I was not the predator, I was the suitor."

"Same thing."

"And besides this, you lured me with your wolf eyes." Here he tapped her leg with his finger. "Did you know that wolves are born with blue eyes? That is correct, blue. But as they mature their eyes turn gray."

"I thought, it was yellow. You should check your source."

"No, you are right, I know this. They can become yellow, yes, or brown or golden, but sometimes they turn gray, like yours."

She shot him a suspicious glance.

"So," he continued, "wolves have gray eyes. But you know I am not a wolf, because my eyes are blue. That means I am a Husky, a dog, and not a predator at all."

"Just a poor KGB infiltrator," she teased, "looking for movies in a movie store."

"No, I was not KGB."

"So, you see me as a wolf, do you?"

"Not exactly," he answered. "I have the confession to make that I see you as a woman, a woman with skin. And that is what we have been talking about, yes? The skin? Your skin?"

"You know," she whispered, returning his tap on the leg, "if I didn't know you better, I'd say you were trying to seduce me, sir."

"But you do know me better, yes?"

Looking directly at his lips, she replied, "Yes, I know you better."

Then, his eyes fixed upon her lips, he said, "No, you are not a wolf, you are a woman with very nice skin, nice legs, nice bottom. So, when can I be kissing it?"

She turned away then and bathed her face in the warm sunlight of Lake Como. Slowly, deliberately, as if weary from repeating herself, she answered him, her eyes upon the distant water, "You can have the woman. But not here, for both of you would be arrested and thrown into prison. And Italian prisons are notorious, like I said. You will have to wait until a more appropriate place presents itself. Then, yes, you may have her."